A STRANGER IN A STRANGE LAND

Joanne had always thought of England as a green, enchanted place, a land of aristocratic life, rich culture, delightful romance.

But now, as she peered through shrubbery at a field illumined by the chill light of the moon, she saw another England—an England as ancient as the Druids, as terrifying as the primal depths of the soul.

There the villagers Joanne knew by daylight as good, God-fearing folk were dancing wildly. Their naked bodies thrashing in the throes of uncontrolled passion. Even as her mind recoiled, Joanne could not turn her eyes from this lascivious spectacle, or from the figure who stood in the center, the lord of the scene, a creature with the powerful, muscular body of a man and the head of a bull.

And despite herself and her disgust, Joanne felt the excitement growing within her, drawing her from safety into diabolical danger. . . .

#8
KATHERYN KIMBROUGH'S
Saga of the Phenwick Women

JOANNE,
THE UNPREDICTABLE

POPULAR LIBRARY • NEW YORK

Dedicated to Terry Wayne

PROLOGUE

How naive I must have been to think I could wield extensive power from the grave. The two dimensions, while not that remote from one another, are of separate vibrations, one little affecting the other. I move freely about, yet always magnetized, as it were, back to Greenfield and Phenwick House. The longitude of my travels, if that is what it may be labeled, is far reaching and I often find myself wandering about remote, unfamiliar places on earth. This is hell, to be so close, yet to be so uninfluential. And to observe my family age and grow old, ultimately to come to this side, often hurts. Now other generations, children who have only heard of me and my notorious reputation, are growing, maturing, carrying on the tradition that I set for the Phenwick women.

But is it worth it? Have my efforts been only vain attempts at achieving immortality?

On the other side of the coin, it is a constant amaze-
ment to me to watch the determination of these Phenwick women. We were not all cut from the same piece
of fabric. Perhaps there is only a germ of similarity in
any of us, still there is no mistaking that determination
that has somehow been injected in those who have come
after me.

Just four years after Danny made his transition and
was himself in the process of progressing beyond, Elias
committed suicide at the altar of the church wherein he
was principal preacher. His hypocrisy had become so
overwhelming, he could no longer abide himself. Once
Rebecca was married, he went quickly downhill, indulg-
ing in forbidden intimacies and having notorious af-
fairs to drown his sorrows over his daughter.

Shortly after Elias' death, Patricia, who had long been
neglected by her husband, but accommodated by a series
of young men vaguely connected with the arts, decided
to wipe away the past. Long she had lamented that Barrywell House had not been constructed on Beacon Hill.
She had it demolished stone by stone, pulverizing each
part in search of hidden treasure. Her search was fruitful and she became exotically wealthy. I regretted that
it was she who found the bulk of my fortune hidden at
Barrywell, yet I knew she had only a limited time left
to enjoy it. The new home on Beacon Hill, which was
more elaborate and modern than Barrywell House, was
beyond my wildest dreams. Patricia was a Phenwick
woman I had to admire and respect.

By spring of 1833, Edward House, as the house on
Beacon Hill was to be known, was complete and a gala
party season was planned.

That winter Johnny Ornby had suddenly taken ill at
Greenfield. By late January Rebecca was a widow. Her

brief, wonderfully happy years of marriage were over and she fell into a pit of depression. Her stepdaughters, Adriane and Lydia, went to Greenfield to stay with her; even their solace could not come close to cheering her.

Joanne Phenwick left La Chenille late that spring. She had been invited to several of Patricia's parties and proved to be the outstanding attraction at each. Shortly after pretty Joanne's most successful debut into Bostonian society, Patricia made arrangements for her niece to visit Susannah in London in early autumn. Joanne was pleased; Patricia was pleased since the former had a way of flirting with several young men whom the latter found particularly attractive. Patricia did not need that kind of competition in her own home.

In all honesty, I must admit I never knew of a Phenwick woman to equal Joanne. She was in a catagory all her own.

CHAPTER ONE

1834

Salty breezes. Sails billowing with wind. Ocean swells. Constant bobbing up and down. Clear blue sky. The sun brightly shining, gleaming off the wooden deck, bits of metal, the masts themselves. The journey from Boston seemed interminable and no semblance of land in sight.

Black flutters of woolen material: outer garments, undergarments and over garments. She had dressed the role of the bereaved widow, the young matron robbed of happiness by her husband's early death. Still tears. Still remembrances. Still unbearable grief. She stood at the rail, the flapping of her black, flowing attire clapping in the wind. Day after day she stood at that rail, staring through transparent black linen toward the horizon, toward England and perhaps toward some diversion from the moribund atmosphere that surrounded her.

Her mother had arranged the voyage, placing her in the company of the grown girls who had suddenly become her stepdaughters with her marriage to Johnny Ornby in 1826. Since neither Adriane nor Lydia Ornby possessed exciting personalities, nor provided stimulating company, Patricia Phenwick had enlisted her niece's assistance for the voyage, thus killing two problems with one trip. And there was no denying that Joanne Phenwick had stimulating characteristics, a bouncy personality and an inquiring nature—to mention a few of her qualities.

Rebecca rarely removed the black veiling from her face. Features had grown coarser over the years, harder over the last few months. Seven months a widow and it seemed an eternity. She had arrived aboard the *Augusta II* in a recluse condition and went instantly to her cabin, where she remained for the first two days. Adriane and Lydia, one or both, were in constant attendance. Since the daughters of Dr. Johnny Ornby were as distressed as the widow, they made a fine trio at sharing grief. Joanne, on the other hand, could barely tolerate being in confined quarters with so much grief, and declared as much to Rebecca and the two girls.

Eighteen, Joanne was highly active, constantly moving, if only wiggling her finger or tapping her toe. A direct blood descendant of the original Phenwick woman, Augusta, she possessed her share and more of that phenomenal hereditary beauty. A cameo of perfection in every feature. Reddish-blond hair and lavender-blue eyes like her paternal grandfather. Her loveliness was often referred to by the faculty at La Chenille School for Girls as pure classical beauty. Joanne honestly thought that was a gross exaggeration, but she blithely accepted the compliment and stored it with the others she received for her extraordinary beauty.

Laughter could not be contained with Joanne; it was prevalent in her speech as if she were perpetually giddy. Because of her high strung nature, the singing laughter was more an inner response; it was infectious. Even solemn Lydia and Adriane could not help but burst into trills of giggles when Joanne set about to make them laugh. The attractive girl was foremost an entertainer. At first she simply desired provoking laughter from her audience, whoever that might be; but in time she learned that people were also entertained by reacting and expressing other emotions. She was, without a doubt, an actress. Eccentricity became purposefully built into her character and she reacted somewhat dramatically to most emotional situations. At a funeral she was the most demonstrative mourner—even for a virtual stranger; as a listener to a humorous tale, she laughed and/or clapped and/or displayed the appropriate reaction, only more so than anyone else did.

Peter Phenwick, now undisputed head of Medallion Enterprizes in Boston, had made arrangements for the trip to England with a dual purpose in mind. First, the obvious purpose of sending the ladies to visit Susannah and Lex; second, to provide chaperones for his two youngest sons on their way to Elton School, a short distance out of London. The boys, Prentise and Joshua, ages 16 and 14, respectively, while well mannered, still possessed some of the same impishness that motivated their sister Joanne. Joshua, particularly, was all boy with a playful attitude that delighted in boyish pranks. Both Prentise and Joshua were handsome lads, with the same prettiness of features that Joanne displayed. In fact there was a remarkable resemblance between the three siblings. Their older brother, Augustus, now twenty, remained in Boston to work with his father. Not interested in an advanced formal education, Augustus chose to learn everything he could from his father in hopes of one day replacing him as the head of Medallion.

Joshua was restless throughout the trip. The few days at sea had bleached his hair nearly white and burst a field of freckles over his face. He helped the sailors, queried the officers about their duties and even took time to know the captain. Together with Prentise, he would climb the masts, the ropes and into every passageway they could find below. Joshua was the instigator.

Joanne had eyed the sailors from the moment she boarded the vessel, making note of at least four who were handsome enough or masculine enough to interest her. She could be a tease, and she was, since the men had been admonished to avoid any and all social contact with the women passengers. There was no avoiding meeting the boys.

So Joanne teased, looked pretty, tormented and caused many a strange dream among the men. If she had only known their innermost thoughts . . .

Thus Rebecca kept her daily afternoon watch at the rail, gazing blankly into the horizon. The cabins below were uncomfortably hot with poor ventilation; she could hardly abide remaining closeted in hers throughout the daylight hours. The tears came less frequently, the soul aching began to lessen. The sea air was good for her, she rationalized, good for her mind and emotions.

"Excuse me, Madame," the uniformed captain said one afternoon three days before their scheduled arrival at London.

Rebecca glanced at him, her features well hidden behind the heavy veil. "Yes, what is it, Captain?"

"Madame has kept so close to her cabin," he continued properly, "that I have not had the opportunity of speaking with you. It is my usual custom, as captain of the ship, to take a personal interest in our passengers. Mr. Phenwick is very emphatic about that. Mrs. Ornby, isn't it?"

"Yes."

"May I first offer my condolences in your time of grief?" he commented. "The loss must be very difficult. But, if I might observe, your cousin tells me you are still a young woman. Wouldn't it be better to remove these widow's weeds and let a little freshness into your life? The sea air has a marvelous way of sweeping out many of the cobwebs in the head."

"I don't know that I'm ready to put away my widow's weeds yet."

"You'll never know until you try."

Rebecca thought a moment. She had always been a sensible person, hardly ever given to extreme emotional reactions. Her marriage to Dr. Johnny Ornby had added a new dimension to her life which, now that it was no longer there, was sorely missed. Resolutely she put her hands to the veil and lifted it from her face.

"Perhaps a bit of sea breeze won't hurt."

The captain stared at her, cocking his head slightly to get different perspective. "Do I know you? That is, have we met before?"

A faint blush. A tiny smile. Her head tilted slightly to the side. Very indistinctly she shook her head.

Anxiously he reached into his inside jacket pocket, fumbling a few moments as if hunting for an object. In a moment, he brought his hand forward and held it before

her. As the fingers uncurled, he revealed a small gold
cross with a gold chain.

"Rebecca?"

She blinked, reaching to lightly touch the bit of jewelry. "Cathcart? Robert Cathcart?"

"You remembered my name."

"You were only a deckhand when last we met," she
said, pushing the veil back even farther.

"You inspired me to want to reach for higher things in
this world," Robert explained. "What has it been? Eight
—nine years? Not a long time."

"Yet a time when so many things happened," Rebecca
stated, wanting to push her bonnet completely back, to
free her hair. "Had I known you were the captain—"

"Ah, had I known you were the passenger." He bowed.
"Would you do the honor of dining with me this evening?"

"I've not been eating much—" She caught herself.
"Yes, of course, I would enjoy that."

Joanne observed the meeting of the two friends from
the past. She wondered what their story was, but she
had a feeling she could perceive what their story would
be. She wanted Rebecca to be happy because she had
been unhappy for so long.

Now the animated young lady was anxious for the
tedious sea voyage to end. The fascination she once had
for the sailors had diminished when she realized they
were forbidden to become friendly with her. She was
certain that was more her father's doing, than the Captain's. Her father knew her too well.

At night she would prowl about the deck on the pretense of watching the stars. Occasionally Joshua would
join her. He was the daring one, too. Prentise was more
the scholar. Together they would make up fantastic sto-

ries about impossible things that could never happen. Then they would laugh at the absurdity of their creations. A bond of closeness was strong between them.

"Until I met you," Joanne overheard Robert Cathcart tell Rebecca the last night at sea, "I was content with my lot, never striving to be anything more than what I was at the time. I had no grand ambitions; no reason to have them. Meeting and getting to know you inspired me to pull m'self up by the bootstraps. I've worked hard to get where I am with no hereditary advantage behind me."

"You've done admirably well, Robert."

"That, coming from you, makes it all worth the while."

"Why should it, Robert? You know your accomplishments." Rebecca had had to admit to herself that she was fascinated with the man. She thought it would never be possible for her to show interest in another man again. Somehow with Robert, the painful memories of the recent past slowly began to diminish. Smiles came when she spoke with him.

"Ay, I know my accomplishments," he replied, "but I also know the motive behind them. And I will be truthful with you, Rebecca, it was all because of you. Oh, I never was so foolish to hope that you and me—I mean— Well, I followed your activities as best I could through Mr. Phenwick and others of the family. Young Augustus was especially informative. Even with your marriage to Dr. Ornby, I never gave up hope. I once had a long conversation with your mother, when she was a passenger for a short journey. A very remarkable woman. I held her attention only briefly since a handsome young sailor captured her interest. Still, she spoke of her concern for you and your well-being."

"My mother is a remarkable woman," Rebecca said

without malice. "We are extraordinarily unalike. She has constructed a fantastically wonderful house on Beacon Hill—a place she has longed to be ever since she first came to Boston. It makes Barrywell House look shabby, and it never was for a moment. I'm glad mother has her new house. She is the *grande* Phenwick *dame*."

"Because of certain work and repairs that have to be made on the ship," Robert advised, "we will be in London dock for three to four weeks, perhaps longer. It's nothing serious, but a 'stitch in time' you know. I thought perhaps I might call on you from time to time, if it would be convenient."

"It would be convenient for me," she remarked, "but I fear it might be an imposition for you to drive all the way out to Merrihew Manor."

"I'll enjoy it. And perhaps there is an inn nearby. I would enjoy spending a few days in the country when I'm not needed here."

Their heads came quite close before embarrassment. Then Robert reached for her hand and raised it to his lips. The memory of Johnny Ornby would never be erased; but with the advent of Robert Cathcart into her life, a new hope began to grow.

"Why don't you marry Captain Cathcart?" Joanne asked later that night when she went to Rebecca's cabin.

"What a thing to ask!"

"You like him, don't you?"

"Captain Cathcart is a very fine man, an admirable man," Rebecca stated, folding her veil as if she intended to put it permanently away. "But I can't even begin to consider such an action so soon after Dr. Ornby's passing."

"Why not? Didn't Johnny want you to be happy?

Wasn't that foremost in his mind?" the girl quizzed snippishly.

"You're only a child, you wouldn't understand this kind of thing," Rebecca reprimanded.

"I'm not a child, Cousin Rebecca," Joanne stated. "Once I left La Chenille I considered myself a full grown woman—an adult. And I know that Captain Cathcart is very much in love with you. You're the only woman he has ever loved, although I cannot imagine why that should be since he is basically an attractive man, a good man and an upright Christian."

"I can't tell if you're flattering me or not."

"Cousin Rebecca," Joanne said, taking her hand, "I only want to see you happy. Your period of mourning seems to be overly long and only has a depressing effect on the rest of us. If I were you I would make a special point of inviting Captain Cathcart to Merrihew Manor."

"I would have to ask Susannah first. My sister is the lady of Merrihew, now, just as I am lady of Phenwick House."

"Then I would make a point of asking Susannah the instant we arrive," Joanne insisted. "Life is too short to waste it lamenting the dead. Be brave, Cousin Rebecca, and you'll find happiness again."

CHAPTER TWO

Three carriages and a livery wagon were waiting at the dock when the *Augusta II* arrived in London. The piers were swarming with activity, excitement, commotion. Stevedores hustled about. Shouts of urgency, orders. Calls from ship to shore, frantic waving. Prentise pretended not to feel the excitement which was causing Joshua to jump up and down like a lad much younger than his actual age. Still both boys were alive with energy and barely avoided several mishaps.

The strikingly handsome woman with dancing blue eyes and golden blond hair remained in the carriage, holding a blue silken parasol above her head. The blue of the parasol matched the hue of her full satin dress. A picture of elegance and refinement, she was more of an attraction than the arrival of the ship. Every sort of person stopped to observe as her equally handsome and distinguished-looking husband alighted from the ornate carriage. Finery suited them so very well, and they knew how to wear it grandly.

Just permitting sufficient shade over her eyes, she watched for the arriving visitors. Not her cup of tea, still she felt obliged to meet the ship and her sister because she had not seen her since Rebecca was a small child. Delicately beautiful Susannah's appearance was deceptive, hiding the fact that she possessed remarkable strength and ability at playing the piano. She was the rage of every salon, of royal society, of the throngs and masses who appreciated pianoforte. Great musicians drank outrageous toasts to her talent; famous artists proclaimed her beauty. Now thirty-three, she radiated the youth of a twenty-year-old. Charm flowed from her and her gracious attitude won compliments and friends wherever she went.

Alexander Phenwick, the conservatively handsome eldest son of Danny and brother of Peter, was solemnly distinguished as he made his way to the gangplank. White temples only focused attention on his comely features. With age he had many of the finely constructed features of his half brother Elias. He welcomed Rebecca as uncle, cousin and brother-in-law. He tried only to see her personality, not plainness of face and awkward bone structure. How difficult to believe that this was his wife's only sister, or that Rebecca was the daughter of Elias, who was almost notoriously pretty for a man; much less the child of ravingly beautiful Patricia Phenwick. His attention went immediately to the Ornby sisters, neither of whom were blessed with outstanding loveliness. Kisses and hugs, words of kindness and greeting; only a phrase in passing about Johnny's death.

Joshua Phenwick stepped forward, shook his uncle's hand, then leapt up to plant a kiss on his cheek. Taken by surprise, Lex reddened a bit and wished that he had been quick-witted enough to have caught the lad in midair and held him for a firmer embrace. Childless, the man had never had close contact with young people. The arrival of his nephews was a new experience and he wished for that contact. Prentise Phenwick stuck his hand forward for a handclasp that held reservation.

"Well now, boys, I am delighted to have you here in London," Lex stated. "Let me see, I've memorized your names, now I've got to put faces with names."

"While you're putting names with faces, Uncle Alexander," Joanne commented as she fluttered down the gangplank, "perhaps you'd better file mine into your memory."

"Joanna?"

Joshua nudged the man. "It's Joanne."

Lex was noticeably impressed and momentarily stammered before he regained his composure. "Mayn't I call you Joanna if I prefer?"

"*Joanna?* Oh, I like the sound of it. So continental and old world," she exclaimed. "I wonder that I never thought of it myself, Uncle Alexander."

"Most people call me Lex."

"Mayn't I call you Uncle Alexander if I prefer?" she mimicked.

They laughed. Joshua laughed too. But Prentise cocked his brow and looked skeptical. His sister's flirtatious ways had not escaped his scrutinizing eyes.

"Tell me about your father," Lex said as they strolled to where the carriages were waiting. "Is Peter coming along one of these days?"

"He said he would be coming over sometime this autumn," Joshua responded. "But I think Gus won't come."

"Gus?"

"Our brother Augustus," Prentise informed.

"Oh, yes, Gus. Come along, my lovely ones, and we'll get you into the proper carriages once you've greeted Susannah." Lex pushed them toward where Susannah was waiting.

The sandy-haired, blue-eyed groom stood beside the horses in an attempt to steady them. The noise was frightening, and the horses were basically country animals. Not altogether plain-faced, the young man of twenty-eight years observed the arrivals and immediately reacted to Joanne's overwhelming beauty. His sensual body was loosely clad, since he had removed his coat with the early September heat and almost overpowering humidity. Those garments he wore clung to his person. He tried not to look as if he were on display, but he was the kind of man who could not help the impressions he caused.

A second young man in his late twenties came scuffing around the carriage. Horse-faced, pale, large-toothed, freckled. He possessed an awkwardly upturned nose, sniffling most of the time more out of habit than out of need. Belching noisily, he poked his associate.

"Hey, Alister, what do ye think o' that?" asked Toby Albright.

Alister Tweedly scratched his head in appreciation. "What I think of *that* would even make me blush."

"Ye wouldn't get nowheres near th' pretty one."

"Maybe yes, maybe no."

"Now the other young'uns," Toby speculated, "they'd be an easy try, now wouldn't they?"

"Go on with ye, Toby. Ye're putting naughty thoughts in me mind."

Alister Tweedly helped the Ornby sisters and Rebecca into the carriage he would drive, taking pains to see to their comfort and introducing himself. The ladies were pleased with his manners and felt confident in his hands.

Joshua and Prentise were loaded into the carriage in which Lex was to ride. Their luggage was also carried with them.

Joanne sat opposite Susannah. An immediate reaction of mutual acceptance set them at ease and chattering over mundane topics.

Robert Cathcart hurried down the gangplank and dashed to the carriage wherein Rebecca was seated. He reached for her hand and kissed it lavishly. Few words were spoken. Then the Captain rushed back to the carriage where Lex was observing his romantic actions, and begged permission to come and call at Merrihew Manor. Lex gave consent.

"Who is that? And why all the excitement?" questioned Susannah.

"That's Captain Cathcart," Joanne replied, "and I believe he is frantically in love with Cousin Rebecca."

Susannah tittered. "In love with Rebecca. Oh, my! I do hope so. Rebecca deserves happiness. And a reasonable time has passed since Johnny's passing. Oh, yes, we must pray for Rebecca and—Captain Cathcart, did you say?"

"Yes. We will pray." Joanne's eyes flashed somewhat mischievously before she turned her attention fully to Susannah.

"Lex will take the boys to Elton," Susannah informed. "He'll be home by midafternoon, which will give the rest of you time to settle in."

The carriages started jerkily. Susannah sat composed as if she could magically maintain her balance even under the shakiest of conditions. Bonnet adjusted on her head, she was prepared for whatever pace the driver wished to set.

Susannah pointed out the Medallion office as they moved up the street leading to the dock. Earlier she had indicated where the original office of Barrywell and Son had been. Now it was a warehouse with a none-too-savory appearance.

Conversation was practically impossible over the cobbled streets of the city and, once in the country, the speed of movement prohibited chatter. The ride would take slightly less than an hour. Ribbons flew along with strands of hair, still it was a delightful experience. The countryside had not yet assumed its autumn colors. Large oaks, maples, elms and many other trees added majesty to the scenery. Harvest had begun. The sun was bright, still a hint of rain was in the air.

Finally a grove of pines intermingled with large gnarled oaks. Heavy shade over the lane. Animals scurrying into the woods. Squirrels freezing to watch the passing spectacle. Song birds. Now pasture lands and cows grazing, calves. Isolated bulls, staked and chained to keep them from each other and the cows. Sheep on a distant meadow. Geese, ducks, chickens, each in their individual groups, clustering in their own excitement. Horses gawking idly into the distance or nuzzling. Dogs of various sorts and descriptions leaving their other interests to come investigate the sound of racing carriages. Barking, biting at one another, jumping.

Alister Tweedly kept a stick on the carriage for the purpose of chasing the dogs away. They all belonged to Merrihew Manor, all dozen or fourteen of them. Most were well trained and minded when told to go away; one or two lingered to be threatened with the stick.

Then came the geese to hiss warning and investigate

the new arrivals. Acting like landlords, the birds were most particular as to who came upon the Merrihew property.

Because of the excitement created by the animals, it was necessary to remain in the carriages until the men had the animals under control.

"What a noisy welcome," exclaimed Joanne, amused at the geese and Toby's inability to control them the instant he wished to do so.

"They become a bit tiresome at times," Susannah remarked, "but they're well worth the trouble. Only a person who knows the property well could sneak beyond the animals day or night."

"Do you have prowlers often?"

Susannah found her handkerchief to touch to her face. "Occasionally. The animals pretty well know who belongs here and who doesn't. I advise you to get to know them as quickly as possible—or plan to remain indoors for the duration of your visit."

Rebecca, Lydia and Adriane were given rooms on the second floor in the west wing of the house; Joanne was assigned to space in the east wing fairly near to Susannah's and Alexander's rooms. Rebecca had complained of fatigue, and the Ornby girls had joined in the complaint. The three begged for naps before tea.

"And you, Cousin Joanne?" Susannah asked.

"I'm far too excited to nap now," Joanne exclaimed. "I would just lie wide awake and toss. Besides, I would like to get to know you and Merrihew Manor before I try to relax . . . unless you care to nap, too."

"Goodness, no. I'm on holiday today, and I don't want to waste it by sleeping."

"On holiday?"

Susannah laughed and invited her cousin into the sitting room adjoining her own bedroom. "I spend six to eight hours a day at the piano. I do not concertize during the summer months."

"Concertize?"

"You know I am a concert pianist, don't you?"

"Oh, yes. But it slipped my mind. I should like to hear you play, Cousin Susannah."

"This evening, perhaps, after supper. Besides, before I go off to Paris on my next tour, you will be subjected to many hours of my practicing. I can't help it. It's a necessity."

Joanne stared out the window. "Merrihew seems to go on forever."

"Close to five hundred acres," Susannah informed. "Lex is attempting to acquire more, which had been part of the original Merrihew estate. So far he has been unsuccessful."

"Did Great-grandmother Augusta build Merrihew, too?" questioned Joanne.

"No. She was born here. Merrihew was built perhaps a hundred years or more before her birth," Susannah explained. "Grandmother Augusta came back years after she left and reclaimed the property. Still she did little to recondition it. From childhood Lex had dreamed of coming here for the restoration. Apparently he heard of it as a child not from Grandmother Augusta, but from Great-uncle Ben Strothart. We've gathered many of the family portraits. Mother had duplicates painted of the family in America, too, including the Kelburns of Alexandria, Virginia. Lex is proud of this old castle, as he calls it. He even has purchased the title of Earl of Merrihew."

The geese came hissing up the lane, wings held high and moving in formation.

"Those geese have a frightening appearance, haven't they?" Joanne commented.

"Just don't let them know you're frightened of them," Susannah warned. "They're bluff only to a point, but they'll test the patience out of you." She moved to the window beside Joanne. "Still it wonders me . . ."

"What does?"

"Here two weeks ago a young peasant girl was killed in the meadow beyond the stable," Susannah said. "Admittedly, the geese nor the dogs don't go into that area often because there is so little activity—still the body was found on the property, murder committed apparently without alarming the animals. Most unusual."

"A peasant girl?"

"By the name of Sara Cornhill. Her father and brother do plowing and butchering in the community, hiring their services where needed."

"A butcher's daughter?"

"Ira Cornhill, the father, is a sometime butcher, since there isn't all that much demand for his killing ability," Susannah related. "He wears many different hats, hiring out hither and yon. Lex offered him a position on the estate, but old Ira refused. He likes his independence, which is admirable. Jim Cornhill—" She paused and glanced vacantly out the window.

"What about Jim Cornhill?"

"What?" Susannah flushed slightly. "Oh, Jim works with his father most of the time. There were other Cornhill children in between Jim and Sara—she was the youngest—but the rest have left home."

"Jim Cornhill is *not* married?"

"No," Susannah whispered, swallowed hard and repeated it louder. "He's a bachelor and claims he's going to remain one."

Joanne crossed away from the window, her eyes searching about the large room, the ancient furniture that had been refurbished and looked quaintly right for the setting. "Do you find him attractive, Cousin Susannah?"

"I beg your pardon?" Susannah twirled about too quickly, nearly losing her balance.

"Jim Cornhill sounds as if he might be an interesting person to know."

"I don't believe that is what you said."

"It isn't. I shouldn't have asked what I did. It was wrong of me. I don't want you think that I am prying into your business."

"You're very perceptive, Cousin Joanne."

The girl immediately rushed to her cousin and flung her arms about her. "Oh, Cousin Susannah, I meant nothing by what I said."

Susannah put her hands on the girls repentant shoulders. She soothed. "I love my husband. He is a good man. I'm a barren woman. At first I did not want to believe that, suspecting that it was Lex who was deficient—and perhaps he is. Still I would not be certain about myself until I found out. Perhaps it was foolish of me, but I encouraged an affair with a Frenchman while on tour several years ago. I still appeared to be barren. Then I became desperate and had another affair and still another, each time with virile men. The fourth time was with a married man who had seven children. I hired him for the experience. Nothing. I never told Lex of my experimenting nor of the results. I think he has guessed, or at least suspected some clandestine activity. I love him all the more for his consideration. Unfortunately, I found that other men were far more exciting and stimulating than my husband. That is why I look at men like Jim Cornhill with a licentious eye. He

does not respond out of respect for Lex. But one day—"
Her words trailed off.

Joanne eased herself from Susannah's hold and returned to the window on pretense of viewing the countryside.

CHAPTER THREE

Merrihew Manor was originally constructed in the seventeenth century, probably in the early half. Legend says that it was intended to be a castle, perhaps for a prince. However, once the plans were drawn up and construction began, it as quickly halted and no work was done for nearly ten years. The royalty for whom it had been designed met an untimely death amid mysterious circumstances.

Ultimately other arrangements were made for the disposal of the property and building began again. The original structure was less than half the size of the present monstrosity, and, at that, it was a large and rambling mansion. Additional construction was done around the beginning of the eighteenth century; and little more had been done to the building until Alexander Phenwick took possession of it approximately twenty years before.

Upon approaching the manor, one is reminded of a

huge sprawling country home with two full floors of
rooms and part of a third floor. The architecture is a mix-
ture of quaint provincial design and gothic castle. Steep-
ly raked roofs and many chimneys give the top an
uneven line. The thick rock walls obviously had been
constructed as protection against fires. One might suspect,
because of the extreme width of the walls, that secret
passageways might be hidden therein. Lex had never
found such passages, which was not to say they did not
exist. There were small windows with even smaller panes
of thick glass, especially on the ground floor. The most
often used portions of the house could be kept comfortably warm in the winter and amazingly cool in summer; other rooms were drafty and impossible to warm.
The third floor rooms were rarely used by the Phenwicks, therefore basically storage places; in winter they
were blocked off to eliminate drafts.

Joanne had no more than left Susannah's room that
first afternoon at Merrihew Manor, than she encountered
the imposing presence of Cyrus Quigg. Brown distant
eyes, expressionless. A cold demeanor as is deemed suitable for principal butler in such a setting. Nevertheless,
he hardly seemed a butler. Bullishly handsome, he
seemed more a professional wrestler or an entertainer
of sorts than a domestic servant. His normally light brown
hair was capped with a powdered wig, large curls on
the side and a pigtail in the rear. Slightly too small for
his big head, it sat precariously. His costume was out of
the eighteenth century: satin knee breeches, snugly fitting; long white stockings and buckles on his shoes; vest
and jacket and ruffled dickey.

Joanne wondered when she saw him if he were hired
because of his ability as a butler or because he aroused
her cousin's prurient interest.

"I am Quigg, Miss," he introduced himself properly, which dispelled some of her suspicion about the man. "Cyrus Quigg. But they call me Quigg. I've been ten year at Merrihew, I have. So if there is anything you would like to know, pray do not hesitate to ask."

Joanne studied him a minute. "Sometimes I have a dreadful memory. Whatever can I be thinking? I forget which room was pointed out to be mine."

Quigg indicated the proper door. "Mrs. Sharlock was to have put your things away, if she has gotten around to it." He opened the door. "Yes, I see the cases are empty. Shall I take them for you?"

Joanne entered the room. Apparently it had been closed up for some length of time. "Air! This place needs fresh air."

The furniture was heavy, carved, probably imported from Spain. Dark wood. The draperies were dusty as was the canopy above the bed. Joanne watched as Quigg jerked at the window to force it open.

"This room requires more than airing," she commented. "All the cloth should be taken down and thoroughly cleaned. I should think it has not been done in at least a century."

"I cannot tell you precisely when the draperies were last cleaned, Miss," he said, his voice slightly husky. "But I will make note of the need."

"It's not my place to give such orders."

"You are a Miss Phenwick, are you not?"

"Yes. But I'm only cousin to the owners."

Joanne admiringly watched Quigg as he lifted the cases and managed to take them all in one load. Her curiosity was aroused. She might find an occasion to mention his name in passing to Susannah and watch for a reaction.

Moments later there came a rapping at her door. Thinking it was Quigg returned, she opened the door with a jaunty attitude and drew back in alarm at the woman standing there. She was easily in her fifties, stoic and grim. Large nose, long with a bump; severe lips; suspicious eyes set deep into dark sockets. Her gnarled hands were tightly folded together at her waist. Attired fully in black with a gray lace cap and scarf about her neck, she created a terrifying impression. Joanne clung to the handle, but stepped back with alarm.

"Forgive the intrusion, Miss Phenwick," she said in raspy tones that insinuated intrigue, "I am the house-keeper, Mrs. Sharlock. I have emptied your cases and was wondering if there was anything further you wished of me?"

Joanne dismissed her with a thank you and closed the door stoutly behind her. With an overly dramatic imagination conjuring images, she had quickly worked herself into a high emotional state. She looked for the dramatic in most situations, but when reality presented a person like Mrs. Sharlock, then a kind of fear began to take over and move through her. She reacted with trembles and without pretended emotions. The immediate solution was to plant herself in the midst of others, examine that reality and relate it to the overall situation. She would soon come to feel quite at home at Merrihew Manor, and make the most of all the props given her.

Lex spent his time between Merrihew and the Medallion office in London. He kept an apartment of rooms in the city, yet managed to spend most of his time in the country, bringing work with him.

Rebecca was restless at Merrihew. Unfortunately she had heard of the murdered Sara Cornhill on the day she arrived and was never able to relax after that. Tension mounted and sleep became close to impossible for her. She was used to large old houses, still she had never been in one the size of Merrihew. Besides, it was in a foreign land and she felt confined to the house. Twice she accepted Alister Tweedly's invitation to go riding; but even her sport was off because of the apprehension she had about the surrounding countryside.

"Susannah, I just don't believe I can remain at Merrihew Manor," Rebecca stated one afternoon the second week she was there. She had recently come in from riding and was dressed accordingly.

"Oh, little sister," Susannah began, "I had hoped that you would like it here and wish to stay at least until I prepared to leave for my tour next month. Naturally you would be free to spend the entire winter if you like."

"No. I could never do that, Susannah. I long desperately to be back at Greenfield. In all my life, it is the only place I was truly happy."

"Yes, when Johnny was alive."

A sigh. Lips bitten. "I—I was happy when I first went to Greenfield, before Johnny came. True, I was happiest with him. I want to be close to where the memory is the nicest."

"And what of Captain Cathcart?" Susannah asked.

"Captain Cathcart is a very fine man. I must admit that I had reservations at first, but now I am convinced he would make a fine—that is—friend."

"You mean husband, don't you, Rebecca?"

"Yes—perhaps. He hasn't broached the subject. And it is so very near to the time Johnny—"

"Nonsense! The dead are dead! You've given sufficient mourning, that's enough. Being so sad and morose will make you old before your time." Susannah paced. "Rebecca, I would dearly love for you to come with me on part of my tour. Paris is lovely. And Vienna! Well, you have to see Vienna to believe it. Then there are many other places throughout Europe. There are parties and famous people."

"I would be so very out of place in such surroundings," Rebecca insisted. "We're so very different when it comes to our ways of life. No, I've decided to return to Greenfield."

Susannah was resigned. "Do what you will, Rebecca. I've simply extended the invitation."

"And I appreciate it. Merrihew Manor is not my way of life. I've had a pleasant visit, but I would like to get home before winter and the bad weather."

"One thing more, Rebecca. What of mother?"

"Mother?"

"The indomitable Patricia Phenwick," Susannah exclaimed.

"I don't comprehend the meaning of your question, dear sister."

"Ah, so very innocent." Susannah paced to the window. "She has demolished Barrywell House in Boston and built her a pretty little palace on Beacon Hill. All well and good. But Mother is clever at some things and clumsy at others. Rightfully we are her only heirs. That house—Edward House, as she calls it—is to be ours, not to be left to one of her gigolos or to one of the other members of the grasping Phenwick family."

"What a way to talk about your family!"

"I only speak this way because there are so many Phenwick heirs. While Barrywell was still in existence, perhaps they would have reason to claim heritage. Now that Edward House is strictly Mother's—well, I think you see what I'm leading to."

"Yes. But I don't understand what we can do."

"When Peter Phenwick arrives, I want him to make arrangements to see that Mother is properly looked after. And you—"

"Why don't you go back to Boston yourself, Susannah, and speak with Mother?"

Susannah pivoted about, tossing her head as she did. "Because Mother and I have never gotten along well. In fact, I would just as soon never have to encounter her again in this life. I don't wish to discuss it." She took a moment to gather herself to the occasion, changing her attitude as quickly as one might change a suit of clothing. Lightly. Smiling. "What about the girls? Lydia? Adriane? Joanne?"

"What do you mean?"

"Will they stay on at Merrihew?"

"I presumed they would return with me. Neither Adriane nor Lydia find Merriwell particularly merry. Fortunately they share the same room or they would never get a night's sleep."

Joanne appeared at the door. "May I come in?"

"Ah, Joanne, come in. We were just speaking of you."

"What have I done now?" Joanne questioned impishly.

"You tell us," Rebecca suggested.

"I'll tell nothing unless I'm found out," Joanne replied gaily. "Oh, I love Merrihew Manor. It's so melodramatic and sinister!"

"What a thing to say, Joanne!" Rebecca exclaimed. "I swear there is a peculiar perversity in you."

Joanne twirled three times around as she spun into the room. "I've decided beyond a doubt that I am going to become an actress."

"An actress? What put that notion into your head?"

"It's been there a long while. Just being at Merrihew has made it become more urgent in my thinking."

"More urgent?" Rebecca sighed. "You speak with her, Susannah."

Susannah laughed lightly and went to place her hands on her young cousin's shoulders. "So you want to be an actress! What better place than London for you to begin."

"Susannah, you mustn't encourage her," Rebecca moaned.

"Why not, if that is what she wants to do?" Susannah hugged Joanne. "Lex knows several people involved in theatricals in London. I've no doubt he can introduce you to the proper people. At least he can make arrangements. I understand they tour about during the summer months and return to London in the autumn. Still something can be arranged."

"Joanne can't remain in London alone," Rebecca stated weakly.

"She'll be with Lydia and Adriane. Oh, I think it's a marvelous idea," Susannah said. "You can all remain here and go to Lex's apartment in London if and when you begin in theatricals. Perhaps you can come to Europe—Paris anyway—while I'm playing. I think my friends would enjoy meeting my American cousins."

"Don't you consider yourself American, Susannah?" questioned Rebecca.

"Yes, but I live in England now." Susannah danced Joanne around the room. "Reconsider, Rebecca. Permit yourself a season of gaiety before you return to dismal Greenfield."

"Greenfield isn't dismal."

"It would be for me." Another twirl about. "We'll make

arrangements. Lex will begin on them the next time he goes into London."

"I'm returning to America as soon as possible, sister. I must go. Besides—"

Susannah released her hold on Joanne and moved curiously toward Rebecca. "Besides?"

"That murdered girl. I have a strange feeling—call it a foreboding—about that. I'm terrified to remain at Merrihew a day longer."

"Oh, Rebecca, at worst the Cornhill girl was trespassing on our property. Chances are she made eyes at the wrong boy in the village and things didn't go as he thought they should. The body was found on our land, but the murder has nothing further to do with us or our house."

"Doesn't it, Susannah?" asked Rebecca as she moved with determination toward the door and disappeared into the hallway.

CHAPTER FOUR

Joanne persuasively convinced the Ornby sisters to remain at Merrihew Manor with her when Rebecca left to return to the United States. Neither Lydia nor Adriane could give adequate reason for remaining in England, only that they had promised Joanne that they would. Rebecca left apprehensively, leaving them with warnings, particularly pertaining to taking chances that might get them into trouble. She did not mention the murder of Sara Cornhill per se, but there was no doubt in any of their minds as to what she meant.

During the three visits made to Merrihew Manor by Captain Cathcart, he became well acquainted with Alexander Phenwick. Lex encouraged him to marry his sister-in-law as quickly as possible, and advised that he do his best to win favor with Patricia Phenwick in Boston. Lex even suggested a marriage ceremony prior to returning to America, but Rebecca had had reservations about it.

Susannah's days were filled with interminable hours of practicing. Her endurance was phenomenal and inspiring, particularly to Joanne. She would sit for long periods listening to her cousin. She had had little exposure to music, with the exception of her Aunt Patricia's musicales to which she was occasionally invited.

Joanne spent a minimum amount of time with Lydia and Adriane Ornby, who occupied themselves with needlepoint and other handwork that could be enjoyed in the quiet of their room. They had begun an ambitious project that would surely take the entire winter and well into spring to finish. Just as well. They had no desire to be out in cold weather. Rebecca had instilled enough fear in them so that they were overly cautious about leaving the house. They retired early with bolted door and remained less than an inch from each other while in bed.

As the Ornby sisters grew suspiciously cautious, they became unwittingly dull. Joanne could barely tolerate their presence at the dining table and was beginning to regret that she had insisted they remain at Merrihew Manor. Perhaps they could be sent on back to New England and she could hire a lady companion to remain with her.

In the meantime Joanne began taking long walks about the property. Her first exercise had been to get acquainted with the animals. Soon she knew the dogs by name and had them eating from her hand. She even gave names to the geese, enduring the initial bruises she sustained from the process of getting acquainted. The hissing creatures seemed to look forward to her company and, when they had not seen her for some time, they would come to the house amid a frightening racket as if to inquire where she was. While not an expert horsewoman as Rebecca was, Joanne quickly acquired a congenial relationship with all but one of the horses. She learned to milk the cows and realized that even sheep react to conversation and kind words. The barnyard creatures became her first audience as she created characters and acted out roles. It can not be said that they were appreciative, but they did show concerted interest.

She had acquired one human among her audience, but she was unaware that he was observing her. Alister Tweedly would crouch in the loft when he would see Joanne coming toward the stable; well hidden, he would watch as she would emote. At times it was all he could do to contain laughter, or applause; and twice her soliloquy nearly brought him to tears, so that he had to rub his nose with the back of his sleeve. The more he watched her, the more he dreamed, conjuring forbidden fantasies. He carried prurient dreams back to his living quarters and did his best to ease the pressure that such created within him.

Finally, one day Joanne had come to the stable to choose a horse for a ride. Alister, prepared for a dramatic interlude, was disappointed. As she was leading the black and gray mare from the place, Alister leaped down from his hiding place, nearly scaring her witless.

"Alister Tweedly! What were you doing in there?"

"I was—that is—I was looking for eggs."

"Eggs in the stable?"

"The hens are known to lay them up in the loft sometimes because of the straw," he informed. "I once found a speckled hen sittin' on eggs up there. She nearly pecked me to death before I could get away."

"Then I shan't disturb you. You may go on with your

egghunt," Joanne replied loftily as she led the horse out into the daylight.

"Miss Joanne—"

"What is it?"

"I've watched you playact," he confessed, following her to the fence. "I see you comin' from the house and I run to the loft and hide to watch. I've aspired to act, m'self, every since I first saw a theatrical performance in London."

"You've seen a theatrical performance?" She was impressed.

"I know a fellow who is an actor, himself. He told me anytime I wanted to come and work around the theatre, I was welcome to come. But what would a country boy like me do in London? I would have to beg for food to eat."

Several times Joanne had run her eyes over the supple person of Alister Tweedly. Muscles defined, others bulging. Sensuous. Still he was a servant. She cleared her throat, then turned to mount.

"I would gladly go riding with you, if'n you're afraid," he said awkwardly when other conversation ceased.

"I can find my way."

"I know some different directions. Ones which I've showed Mrs. Phenwick from time to time."

Joanne stared down at him. "Susannah?" She controlled a smile. From the angle she was sitting she could realize that Alister Tweedly was indeed a desirable man who might have well captured her cousin's romantic interest.

Alister looked down. "Would Miss Adriane and Miss Lydia be in their room, then?"

"Lydia? Adriane?" Her suspicions were magnified. Surely her old maidish cousins had not encouraged the groom. She was of the impression that they were hardly aware that men existed. "We'll speak later, Mr. Tweedly. One side! I wish to leave."

Alister watched as she raced her horse down the path, four hounds barking merrily behind her. She was developing into a fine horsewoman, riding like a lady of class and breeding.

Two dogs, named Jaspar and Alonzo, mongrels of dubious past, followed along with her after the other two lost interest. When fully out of vision from Merrihew Manor, she reined up and dismounted. The dogs lapped large tongues over her before she managed to escape their affection and mount again, this time straddling the horse as a man does. She would ride ladylike in public, but the way she pleased in private. Besides she could make better speed in such a position. The dogs soon tired. First Alonzo lingered behind, then Jaspar as Joanne rode into a denser part of the forest.

Ten minutes later, tree limbs wildly reaching for her, she lost the path which was covered with fallen leaves. The bright colors of autumn were still in full force, but the carpet of leaves was becoming thicker and thicker. Finally she pulled up. Was she actually lost? She could not see the sun, nor shadows cast by it. Only a twinge of apprehension. Curiosity. Where had her ride brought her? Was it still part of the Merrihew estate? Reversing her direction, she walked ahead of the horse. She tried calling for Alonzo and Jaspar, even whistling, but received no response from the dogs. Twice she found cleared areas which might have been trails, but upon following them, she wound up at impasses. Deeper apprehension. Worry. She was caged in by the forest. Surely there must be a way out. How had she missed it?

Nearly an hour later she was wandering fruitlessly

about. Twice she had mounted the horse and told him to go home; but he remained in place, looking back at her as if he questioned her sanity.

Forest animals scampered. A large stag approached. She held perfectly still until he got nearly to her. The horse made a noise, the wild animal fled. Moments later a gunshot. Joanne rose and went in the direction of the sound. But the forest was deceptive and sound echoed, appearing to be everywhere at once. She called out. Another report. Perhaps the stag had got away.

Leading the horse, she moved in the direction she thought the sound had come from. That took her through heavy thickets. She went back and sat exhausted on a fallen tree trunk. Untying her hair, she let it flow down as she brushed her fingers through it to comb the bits of twigs and leaves that had gathered there. Arranging her skirts so they would not drag on the ground, exposing her legs, she went to the stream for water. Apprehension had developed into fear, and that had created a thirst. Squatting before the trickle of water, she had to push the leaves aside to get her cupped hands sufficiently filled with water.

Upon rising from the stream, she turned back with an astonished gasp. Standing a short distance from her was the hunter whose volley she had heard. Broad shoulders. Ruggedly good looking in a country-boy way. Thickly built with hunting clothing that fit snugly to him, magnifying the musculature beneath. Large boots indicated his feet were bigger than most men's. He doffed his cap, a bush of brown hair falling over his forehead. A smile larger on one side of his mouth than on the other; teeth showing. Impudent laughter, licentious, mocking. Legs apart, he stood with his hands on his hips in an accentuated masculine pose.

Joanne stared at him for several moments, neither moving nor breaking the silence beyond his periodic chuckles. Realizing her skirts were still hoisted, she quickly untied them and let them fall to the ground.

"Is the little exhibition over?" he questioned in husky tones, coarse and somewhat inarticulate speech.

"I am not on exhibition!" she fired back, advancing toward him as if she intended to battle over his one statement. "I happen to be lost and I was refreshing myself from the stream."

"I found it refreshing, meself." He laughed boisterously, not altering his position.

Joanne moved closer, getting a better look while she worked her dramatic ability into an irritated response. "I care neither to be ogled nor laughed at. I demand to know what you're doing on the Phenwick property."

"Ye've o'erstepped the Phenwick property, lass," he returned, leaning back as he chuckled. "It ended back a way. This is free land, public forest."

"Were you the one who shot at that stag?"

"Ay, I shot at him, but me aim was off. Had ye not cried out, I would 'ave 'ad 'im, though." He swaggered closer, accentuating his image of masculinity. "I take it that ye are a Phenwick by birth or persuasion."

"I am. Joanne Phenwick."

"Joanne, is it? Well, now, this is a right pretty name, lass." He wiped his hand thoughtfully over his virile-looking face and down to pat about his tight belly. "I've never known a lass by the name of Joanna before."

"Joanna? You mean—no, I like the way you say Joanna," she said, puzzled at the reaction she was beginning to have toward the man, one which made her pretended dramatics difficult to continue. "Who are you?"

"I'm just a wee farm lad out doin' a bit of hunting," he returned.

"Wee?"

"I meant the farm is wee. What did ye think?" He roared with merry laughter, concluding by nearly reaching out to slap her playfully in the process. Managing to control his urge, he laughed even harder.

Aware of what his intentions had been, and the expression he momentarily formed when he caught himself, Joanne was also amused. She giggled girlishly. Near enough to the horse, she reached out and caught his reins.

"Ye're lost, aren't ye?" he asked at length.

"Confused."

"Ay, I'll agree to that. And for your information, ye're the one what's oglin', not me—well, perhaps a might." Again laughter.

"I was not ogling you. Ladies don't—"

"Don't? I do nay agee with that."

"I was merely sizing up your character," she explained weakly.

"And what do ye think o' me character, lass?"

"Impudent! That's what I think."

"Gi' us a kiss an' I'll show ye the way out of here."

"I don't kiss strangers."

"Ay, just one kiss."

"I—that is—I don't even know your name."

"It's Jim."

"Jim? A common name."

"Ay, that it is. Jim Cornhill is me full name."

"Jim Cornhill. Cornhill?" A startled expression. "Oh, you're—I mean."

"Ay, I'm the son o' Ira Cornhill and brother to the dead

girl, Sara." Large feet stepped nearer to where she was standing.

"Oh, I am sorry." She wanted to reach out and touch him.

"Ye needn't be sorry. 'Tis the lad what killed her what ye need to be sorry for," Jim exclaimed.

She viewed him compassionately, then from another point of view. In a moment she had stepped to him. Their eyes met. Up on her toes, she managed to reach her lips to his cheek. The kiss was quick and she was in the process of lowering back to the ground when he wrapped his arm about her and pulled her back to his face, this time positioning her so that their lips met. Strong grip. Lips that tasted rough, but large and inspiring. He approached hungrily, then lessened his intensity. Using both hands, he gripped her about the waist and slowly lowered her to the ground. Dusting his hands on the seat of his trousers, he sheepishly lowered his head.

"I swore I would never do that to unsuspectin' lasses again until I found me sister's killer," he said.

Her lips were still vibrating with excitement. "Never again?"

"Some lout took advantage o' me sister, Sara," he continued contritely. "I'll not be a similar lout meself."

Their eyes met. Joanne seemed to be asking so many questions with her eyes, questions that would never be verbalized. She tried to smile, but her lips just got pouty and quivered as if they desired another taste of his.

"Climb aboard your horse, lass, and I'll lead ye out o' here," Jim ordered.

When she stood as if paralyzed, he stepped forward and reached to give her a hand. Stubby fingers quivered as he wanted to place them again about her waist, instead he hooked the fingers together and made a stirrup into which she could step.

Moments later she was back atop the horse. Again their eyes met as he let his hand casually follow down the turn of her leg. The same hand reached for the reins.

"I'll lead ye back onto the path."

"Jim?"

"Ye'll be wanting to get home before dark."

Jim Cornhill led the horse back to the trail and indicated the way back to Merrihew Manor.

"Thank you," she said softly as Jim handed the reins to her.

"'Twas me pleasure, lass. Ay, indeed it were."

"Perhaps we'll—"

"Perhaps ye had better git on with ye, Joanna. Ye don't want to think much o' the likes o' me. Go on, now, and God be with ye."

Jim turned and trudged his way back into the forest. Joanne waited a few moments, watching the man with the broad shoulders and swagger that could never be disguised. And her lips still tingled from the texture of his.

CHAPTER FIVE

The night before Susannah and Lex's departure for Europe and the start of the concert tour, a grand party was planned by friends in London. Susannah was to be the guest of honor. Supper for eighteen with royalty among the guests. The hostess, aware of Susannah's cousins from America, included the three girls as guests. The excitement of that day could hardly be contained. Adriane and Lydia had been to other parties, but none which promised the appearance of royalty. It would be like a fairy tale coming true. Even Joanne was a bundle of excitement and confusion.

Since Susannah would be playing that evening, not a full concert but a preview of what her continental audiences were going to hear, she left word that she was not to be disturbed. Her personal maid, who had been away for the summer, returned, and she was the only one permitted in the mistress's room until the carriages were prepared for the journey. Even Lex was forced to remain in his own quarters or rummage about the house on his own. The maid, Marie Antoine, was in her thirties and had raised a family between her domestic duties. The family lived in France. Marie had come to England only for final preparation with her mistress.

Joanne had had a white satin gown made for the occasion, having sent for the dressmaker to come from London to measure and fit. Even Susannah did not know what the pretty girl had planned.

The Ornby sisters intended wearing dresses they had worn in the past to a formal party or two and to one of Patricia Phenwick's salons—the only one to which they were ever invited. They would look dowdy but presentable; and they would be ignored, or overlooked, or avoided.

Susannah wore lemon yellow, her favorite color, with trim of white lace. The bodice was low cut and revealing; the skirt was bouffant, the sheen of the satin glistening with clusters of rhinestones. White gloves over which she would wear diamond bracelets. A glorious diamond necklace would rest between her throat and her bosom —a special gift from Lex for the occasion. Because of threats of highwaymen, the jewelry was kept in a vault in London. It would be donned at the last minute.

Because of the width of their skirts, Susannah and Joanne had to ride in separate carriages, while Adriane and Lydia rode together with Marie Antoine. Lex left early so that he might get the jewelry from the vault.

Joanne wore two diamond bracelets, gifts from her brother Augustus when she left for England. Because they were sparkly, but not of great value, she kept them with her at Merrihew Manor. However, as her carriage pulled up before the house where the party was to be given, Lex appeared at the door and handed her a package.

"What is it, Uncle Alexander?" Joanne gushed.

"A special gift for you, Joanna," he replied. "Your father asked me to purchase it for you."

"My father?"

"Excuse me, I must get to Susannah. You will enter after we do," Lex informed, anxious not to detain his wife.

Joanna watched as Lex helped the beautiful Susannah from the carriage, several footmen in attendance to catch her gown to keep from dragging across the ground. She could hear them being announced and watched as they entered. Moments later footmen appeared at her carriage. She had them wait while she opened the package and beheld the most gorgeous diamond necklace she had ever seen.

"May I be of assistance, Miss Phenwick?" came the familiar voice.

Joanne glanced up into the handsome face of Cyrus Quigg, who for once appeared to be wearing a wig of the proper size. Standing there in his ivory satin uniform, he reminded her somewhat of Jim Cornhill: same bulky build and obvious masculinity.

"Oh, it's you, Quigg," she said, somewhat startled to see him.

"I was your driver, Miss."

"Aha! So that explains the expert ability with which the horses were handled."

"You compliment me."

"Not unjudiciously." Her eyes swept over the man. Why did he always make her slightly nervous, restless? Yet intrigued. The satin uniform clung to him, glistening over thick muscles, although he appeared somewhat awkward in knee breeches. "Yes, you can assist me. I'm having difficulty with this catch."

Quigg climbed into the coach, doing his best to step over Joanne and avoid physical contact. That was next to impossible. Other times they had inadvertently rubbed past one another, fleeting moments of contact that were startling at best if not stimulating. He sat on the seat beside her as she turned her back to him.

"Perhaps if you unloosen your cape, Miss."

She did, letting the white woolen cape with the silver gray fur trim fall part way down her back. His fingers were large but clever. Avoiding touching her bare neck as much as possible, he made the clasp work. Then he permitted his fingers to faintly touch as they moved down to lift the cape back to her shoulders. A moment later he was climbing over her again; a singular move since he could have just as well used the other door.

"Gather your skirts, Miss," Quigg instructed as he motioned for footmen to come assist.

Hands reached, some touched. It was all part of the action required for such a movement. The skirt and the long cape did not touch the ground as her attendants helped her to the door. She glanced back at Cyrus Quigg as if she expected him to continue with her into the house. He was staring at her in a strange way—an interested way, she thought. Merely nodding approval, he turned slightly to give instructions to the footmen.

Ivers Palace, belonging to Lord and Lady Archibald Smilington, was really a large townhouse of mansion proportions. The furnishings were opulently grand with many mirrors, crystal baubles and flickering candles everywhere. The guests were greeted in the ballroom, which was generally used as a reception area. Since the Phenwicks were the last arrivals, timed to be noticeably

late, Susannah's entrance on Lex's arm was spectacular.
A more handsome pair could not be found in all of
London, if in the world. Susannah was elegance itself,
the very last word in sophistication and grand manners.
Men immediately sailed across the room to get a closer
look, and women eyed her with envy. Lady Ophelia
Smilington, a tall woman with a long face and a distinguished nose, extended the first hand in greeting.
Her richly melodic voice rolled forth in deep tones. A
hush fell over the others as if they wished to hear the
words exchanged between the two. Lord Archibald
Smilington, paunchy, short and balding, hastened to his
wife's side. Apple-cheeked, he bubbled with a giggling
quality that was amusing and somewhat annoying. An
aristocratic member of the artistic society of London, this
middle-aged connoisseur wished of all people to impress
Susannah Phenwick. Her presence in his house was considered a rare honor, and an event about which he could
brag at his club in days to follow.

Once the host and hostess had greeted the honored
guests, Lex and Susannah were escorted about the room
and introduced to others. While they were chatting with
Lord and Lady Henry Weston, near neighbors to Merrihew Manor, a sudden silence fell over the room. They
all turned toward the entrance where Joanne was standing. Elegance, absolute perfection of beauty, a rare combination of youth and sophistication. Turning her head
from one side to the other, her face was like a cameo
created by the most talented artist and specialist in
feminine beauty. Gasps. Sighs. A distant exhaling of
breath that sounded almost like a whistle.

"Lovely! She's absolutely lovely!" Lady Smilington exclaimed. "I don't know her name, but what a marvelous
distraction for one's party."

"Who is she, my dear?" Lord Archibald asked as he wedged in between his wife and Susannah.

A feeling of pride mixed with uncertainty crept through Susannah. She concentrated on avoiding a haughty expression, and covered it with a gregarious smile that she had long before manufactured for hiding her emotions in public. "She is my cousin, Miss Phenwick."

"Miss *Joanna* Phenwick," Lex added from the other side of his wife. He was beaming proudly at his niece.

Lady Ophelia made a sign to the head butler standing beside Joanne. Lex and the girl exchanged glances.

"Miss Joanna Phenwick!" the butler announced.

A murmur of chatter ran through the room. Lex strode across the area and reached for Joanne's hand. He bent forward and kissed it, before he led her to her host and hostess.

Moments later Lydia and Adriane Ornby entered, creating little or no disturbance whatsoever. Announced, they received only curious glances, which did not linger. Lex again made the trip to the entrance and gathered his cousins by the arms and directed them to meet Lord and Lady Smilington.

For the next several minutes Lex was occupied with introducing the young ladies to different guests. Lord Archibald took it upon himself to personally show Joanne about, introducing her and relishing the thought of having such a beautiful creature on his arm.

The young man of aristocratic attitude and disposition, standing by the piano, observed the entrance with indifference. Long, well-formed nose; gray eyes with lids half covering them; long angular face with a sharply protruding chin: all joined together to make it appear as if he were looking down upon the world, which he did most of the time. His skin was light, although he still maintained the blossom of youth which gave color to the pampered, spoiled attitude that seemed to permeate his otherwise handsome features. For nearly three years he had had a secret longing for Susannah Phenwick. It frustrated him to see a young woman so beautiful and talented so unavailable and obviously in love with her husband.

"Tark, may I present Miss Joanna Phenwick?" Lord Smilington asked as he lavishly displayed the pretty girl. "This is A. Tarkington Quilby. We call him Tark."

Joanne felt a clamminess in the texture of the young man's hand. She controlled blushing at the intensity with which he stared at her. Perhaps it was a mistake wearing her neckline so low that it exposed part of her chest.

"There will be dancing later, Miss Phenwick," Tark managed to say in garbled tones. "I trust you will save one for me."

"I would be honored," Joanne returned simply because he was the youngest man present and one of the few unattached. "And I hope you will find it in your heart to dance with my cousins as well. If you would, I might be inclined to consider a second dance with you."

Without scrutinizing the cousins, Tark agreed.

While Joanne was still smiling at Tark Quilby, Lord Smilington pushed her toward the Tatterwigs. Justin Tatterwig was an attorney and a man about town. Tallish, he was severely handsome in a conservative way. Dark hair and eyes, he had a penetrating gaze that instantly made young ladies feel ill at ease. His wife, Clarice, was a portly woman with an enormously round face, flat features and a high and extensive bosom. Voice a bit shrill and piercing. Reddish hair. Dull gray eyes when they could be seen beneath corpulent eyelids.

"Oh, my dear! What a gorgeous entrance!" Clarice Tatterwig shrieked. "Wasn't it simply gorgeous, Justin? There, you see. I have never seen anything so overwhelming. Visiting royalty, that's what I thought you were. That's what I thought she was."

"Thank you, Mrs. Tatterwig," Joanne said politely and nudged Lord Smilington.

"Justin has double-jointed knees," Clarice went on, "but he is a passable dancer. Perhaps you would do him the honor."

Joanne glanced at Justin Tatterwig. An impish exchange of smiles. She nodded and allowed Lord Smilington to lead her forward.

"You know Lord and Lady Weston, don't you?" questioned Lord Archibald as they approached the couple who appeared to be in their mid-forties. "He's Lord of Weirwyck. Falcon Heath Castle is only a short distance from Merrihew Manor. You're practically neighbors."

Lord Henry Weston was a huskily handsome man with a moustache and rosy cheeks. Blondish red hair, turning to gray, deep blue eyes with a whimsical twinkle. A space between his front teeth and the beginnings of jowls beneath his sideburns. Still he was quite good looking.

"Had I known we were neighbors, Miss Phenwick," Henry Weston remarked, "I think I should have considered being more neighborly prior to this."

Lady Genevieve Weston cleared her throat.

"Oh, yes, my dear, quite so."

Hazel eyes peered down at Joanne. Bored but pleasant, the sharp line of her mouth forced a smile as she seemed to line a person up by the tipmost part of her sub-

stantial nose. "Lord Henry is perfectly harmless, my
dear. He's a dreamer."

"That's what she thinks," Lord Henry muttered.

"How's that?"

"Nothing, my dear. Nothing."

Joanne enjoyed the attention shown her, the responses
she aroused, the flattery, the ogling glances that insinuated more than words dare to say. She was suddenly
at ease as if she realized that she had conquered the
gathering and now they were hers to do with as she
pleased. Even the ladies, who suspected their husbands
of erotic thoughts inspired by the young lady, were
charmed by her gregarious personality, her personable
smile, her pleasing disposition. Once left on her own,
she mingled well and created excitement wherever she
went.

"Are you someone important?" she asked of a large
man with a fringe of red hair around his bald pate. Large
walrus moustache and bright red heavy eyebrows gave
his face a distinction few men displayed that evening.
Beady gray eyes twinkled out between slits of eyelids.

"Not of much importance, child. I feel terribly awkward in formal attire and not altogether comfortable
among such splendid aristocrats," he replied in a thick
voice with a throaty quality.

"Not aristocratic," she said snippishly, "then you can't
be of importance."

"Not if that is your criterion for importance."

"It's nice but not all that important."

"I'm glad to hear that."

"I'm Joanne Phenwick—correction, Joanna Phenwick."

"You mean you're actually Joanne, but you're affecting
the pronunciation of your name?"

Joanne laughed. "Yes. My Uncle Alexander calls me

Joanna. Perhaps I would have been named Joanna if anyone had thought about it. Who are you?"

"The name's R. Piedmont Stopp. I'm usually called Inspector Stopp, but you may call me Piedmont, if you wish." The man of forty-five blushed in the girl's presence.

"Inspector?"

"With Scotland Yard." He indicated her necklace. "It is because of the likes of that that I've been asked to be here this evening. A rash of robberies in the neighborhood, you know."

"Robberies?"

"Ay. It's not my usual specialty, but I was available. Would you do me the honor of dancing later on? I'm suposed to ask someone and you're the only lass that altogether appeals to me."

"Why, I'd love to." She thought a moment, her natural flirtatious ways undisguised. "What is your usual specialty, Piedmont?"

"Murder."

"Murder!"

"Shh. Not so loud."

Dinner was announced and the guests filed into the large dining room. Because he was handy, Joanne permitted Piedmont Stopp to escort her in. However, they were soon separated as Lady Smilington designated the seating arrangement and Joanne found herself seated between Tark Quilby and Lord Weston.

After dinner, the guests returned to the ballroom where chairs had been arranged around the piano. Susannah presented nearly an hour of piano pieces to the unanimous acclaim of all present. Champagne was passed and the lovely lady was toasted as an outstanding performer and international beauty.

Chairs were cleared away when the concert was completed, and dancing began. A small orchestra sat on the balcony, and the ballroom filled with the swirling patterns of dancers.

Tark Quilby managed several dances with Joanne, who more and more had come to fascinate him. She had come to fascinate others as well. Because Susannah refrained from extensive dancing, it was generally acclaimed that Joanne was indeed the belle of the ball and the most sought after by the men.

Lydia and Adriane accepted several invitations to dance, but neither were accomplished in fancy footwork. Still they made an effort and, since not all of the men were that fleet-footed, they proved to be satisfactory.

Before leaving the affair, Lex collected his wife's and Joanne's jewelry and deposited them with R. Piedmont Stopp, who would see that they were returned to their proper vault.

The evening was successful, and Joanne left with a standing invitation to be further introduced into London society.

Susannah was pleased that Joanne had been so well accepted. She could not even feel envy for her beautiful cousin, only happiness.

While the other carriages returned to Merrihew Manor, their occupants exhausted from the exhilarating activities of the evening, Lex and Susannah went to his apartment in the city, from where they would leave the following morning for the continent.

A strangeness seemed to hover over Merrihew Manor as the cousins arrived back without Lex and Susannah. A mystery settled about, with an almost ominous feel to it. Adriane and Lydia huddled close together as Joanne walked ahead of them, her bouffant skirt requiring space. Mrs. Sharlock would help Joanne first, then go to assist the other girls.

A pair of eyes watched and speculated.

CHAPTER SIX

The following week, when news arrived that Lex and Susannah had successfully established themselves in Parisian apartments, Joanne had already become slightly restless at Merrihew Manor. While Lydia and Adriane had their handwork to keep them fully occupied, Joanne had nothing to absorb her interest. Reading. Occasionally riding; but the weather was more and more becoming touched with the sting of chilliness. The cold chapped her face. Besides she was not all that enthusiastic about horses, not unless in the company of a dashing young man. More and more she observed Alister Tweedly and/or Toby Albright with a speculative eye. Indeed Alister was good looking enough to cause provocative thoughts in her fantasies; still he was only a groom. Often she would engage him in conversation, much of which was shaded with double entendre that eluded Alister. He had had experience in London while in his early twenties, when his boyish handsomeness attracted the attention of a theatrical impresario. Because of that experience, Joanne found Alister interesting, and she often persuaded him to relive that time for her. The extent of his stage experience was the changing of sets while in costume and occasionally carrying a prop that made him appear to be part of a crowd.

"Don't you ever miss the theatre?" questioned Joanne one dark overcast afternoon a short while after returning from a brief gallop.

"I don't think so. It was never deeply ingrained within me," Alister replied.

"Oh, I'm certain if I only once stumbled onto stage, with the flickering lanterns at my feet, that I would never get it from my system," Joanne declared. "Still I would not settle for merely carrying a property and being one of a crowd. I will be the leading lady, with the most elegant costume and all the emotional scenes."

Alister laughed.

Quigg came from the house. His wig, as usual, was at an awkward angle for his large face as if it had been clapped on in haste.

"There is a caller, Miss Phenwick," he announced, his face curiously insinuating suspicion. "He has asked specifically to speak with you."

Grandly Joanne made her way from the stable up the path to the house. Quigg followed a respectable distance behind her, cautiously looking about as if he expected to see strangers lurking about the property.

Joanne sailed into the grand hallway from the rear of the building. Heavy shadows. Only faint light coming through the few windows. Her steps whispered over the wooden floors. Stopping a moment before she reached the parlor, she inspected her appearance, removing the riding hat and cape. Blue dress with white trim was devoid of bouffant underskirts to facilitate ease in riding. Still, as always, she presented a fresh and appealing picture of lovely young womanhood. She had perfected her movements, her gestures, the nuances of graceful positioning of her hands, always aware of creating a pretty posture.

To her surprise, the man waiting for her was R. Piedmont Stopp, the man from Scotland Yard she had met at Lord and Lady Smilington's party. Wearing a tweed suit and cap, he had a rustic look about him that was in direct contrast to the impression he had made the last time she saw him. The cap removed, his shiny dome was haloed with afternoon light coming through the window.

"Ah, Miss Phenwick!" He rushed toward her with extended hand. "You will forgive me for coming without a previously arranged appointment, but because of your distance from London, making such an arrangement would be quite difficult. I took the chance that your hospitality would be generous and I could take a few moments."

She was so delighted to see a different face at Merrihew Manor, that she instantly insisted that he have a seat, and offered refreshment. Tea was decided upon and Quigg was rung for.

"The Alexander Phenwicks are safely arrived in Paris I understand," he commented in opening remarks.

"Yes. We received word just yesterday. Susannah's first concert is to be this weekend."

"A beautiful, brilliant pianist. And I know nothing about music," Stopp commented. A finger in the air. "One cup of tea and I must be off."

"You rode out all this way for merely one cup of tea."

"Not merely one cup of tea, my dear," he explained.

Quigg entered with the tea things and efficiently served. The only unusual thing Joanne noticed about his entrance was the fact that his wig was sitting remarkably straight upon his head.

"Fact of the matter," Stopp said after the butler had left the room, "I have been called up here by Constable Sedley Jones, your local man. Looking after priceless diamonds isn't my usual line of police work, as I've told you before. I'm in homicide most of the time.

"No doubt you've not been spared, at least word in passing," he continued, "about the Cornhill girl who was found murdered in the pasture."

"Sara Cornhill, wasn't it?"

"Yes, to be precise. I've had a talk with her father and brother this afternoon. Frankly, there is fear that if the authorities don't solve this thing, the Cornhills will take matters into their own hands. Such emotionalism could result in disastrous circumstances. They want revenge and they want blood."

"They must have some suspicions as to who the killer might be," Joanne remarked. "Or would they take the blood of an innocent just to satisfy their savage revenge?"

"That would be difficult to say, Miss Phenwick. Thus, I can but ask your indulgence in this matter," he said. "And if you see anything suspicious about, send one of your men immediately to Scotland Yard or to Constable Jones."

"I don't know what you might consider *suspicious*, Mr. Stopp. But if I see anything out of the ordinary, I'll get word to Mr. Jones immediately."

The subject drifted from alarm about Sara Cornhill's murderer or murderers to more refined topics. Joanne found the police inspector to be a witty man and an encyclopedia of tales. He exuded much charm in his garrulous way that, were he a younger person, she might have suspected that he were a suitor. Would that be so far from wrong? After all, he was a handsome man, unmarried, and with a way that aroused a sensual response.

When Joanne invited Inspector Stopp to supper, he declined the invitation, saying that he was not aware of the lateness of the hour and had to leave because of other plans. He was staying at the village inn, where he fortunately obtained the last empty room available.

Even as R. Piedmont Stopp left Merrihew Manor, the northern skies had turned storm black and the rest of the heavens were covered with dark gray turbulence. Distant lightning. The scent of rain. Growling thunder.

"If you don't make it to the village," Joanne said as she stood by the carriage, "please feel free to return and spend the night here, Inspector Stopp."

He took her hand. "Thank you for the offer, my dear, but I'm certain we can make it before the skies fall." He kissed her hand, the hairs of his moustache tickling.

Joanne speculated about the policeman. Perhaps she really found him fascinating because he was familiar with the city of London and claimed to personally know several theatrical innovators. In fact he had promised to take her for an evening of theatre and dining in the near future—weather permitting.

Lydia and Adriane had observed the large blustery man with the moustaches and heavy eyebrows. Neither considered him a romantic figure, still they had both heard that bald men of middle age were considered by some as extremely handsome. That had been Rebecca's opinion; but perhaps that was because Captain Robert Cathcart was well on his way to that state.

A roaring fire blazed in the fireplace of the dining room. A chill had come with the storm. Much fire was required to heat the large, high-ceilinged room. The three young ladies dined together, all seated at one end of the table nearest the fire. By then the storm was raging with severe winds pounding rain against the windows. The draperies were drawn to keep the lightning from startling them; but the cacophony of thunder paralyzed both Ornby sisters with its violent sound.

"I have no more appetite," Lydia declared.

"I have no more appetite for food, nor for England," Adriane responded. "I don't know why we ever allowed you to persuade us to remain in this dreadful place, Joanne."

"My father will come one of these days," Joanne retaliated, "and you can return to America with him. It would have been meddlesome of you to have gone back on the same ship with Rebecca and Captain Cathcart."

Another clap of thunder interfered with their retort to the remark. Adriane rose and went to the chair wherein Lydia was sitting. "Sister, I'm afraid. Perhaps we should retire to our room, climb under the covers and bury our heads."

Lydia stood up to console her sister. Both young ladies were noticeably trembling.

"Do whatever you wish," Joanne stated. "Supper has not been completed. But I will excuse you and finish by myself."

At that moment the great door to the dining room swung open as if the action were riding the crashing sound of thunder. The Ornby sisters jumped with alarm and squealed at the same pitch. Joanne, calmly in control, remained at her place without glancing toward the door until she heard Quigg's familiar footstep.

"Yes? What is it, Quigg?" asked Joanne as if she were playing a theatrical role.

"Begging your pardon, Miss Phenwick," the bulky butler replied, "but a man has arrived in a carriage which appears to be well battered by the storm. They have lost their way and fear, with the condition of the carriage, that they will not make it to the village tonight."

"They?"

"The gentleman and his manservant, Miss. Will you speak with the gentleman?"

"Show him into this room, Quigg," Joanne replied. Even before the butler left the room, she turned to her cousins. "Lydia, Adriane, you may go to your room if you frantically wish, but I would prefer that you remain here with me—at least for the interview of this stranger."

"How can you let a stranger into the house, Joanne?" questioned Adriane, pulling away from her sister and leaning over the table to address her cousin.

"The man is in trouble. It's a terrible storm," Joanne returned coolly. "If you would feel safer in your room, go instantly."

"No," Lydia said, "we'll stay. At least until we ascertain that he is a suitable sort of man."

"That he is a gentleman," Adriane augmented.

"Your concern is greatly appreciated, dear cousins."

The door opened, again timed to the shattering of thunder. The man had removed his hat and cape, therefore appeared basically dry except for his boots. A more dashingly handsome man had not been presented at Merrihew Manor to the three young ladies. Long comely face. Sharp nose and finely formed features. Curly black hair at a debonair length. Penetrating brown eyes. He walked with a grand carriage and gallantly made broad gestures as if presenting himself into a sixteenth or seventeenth century French court.

"M'ladies!" A grand bow, another sweeping gesture with his hand. "Permit me to introduce myself. I am Matthew Bienville. I am now coming from Edinburgh, Scotland. I occasionally make this trip, but I was detained later in the season than usual, thus encountering this sordid weather."

"Your name sounds French," Joanne commented.

"It is French," the man with flashing white teeth announced. "Alas, I am but a sixteenth or a thirty-second Frenchman, practically in name only."

"Are you," Lydia began, then hesitated, "are you a noble?"

"There again, I have royal blood," he admitted, "but only about a sixteenth or a thirty-second. My father is a successful merchant and importer. There is more wealth to be made in being a businessman rather than being royalty. Among other things, I invest and sponsor various aspects of the arts, including the theatre; although that worthy endeavor doesn't always fall in the category of the grand arts. One day, mind you."

"Sponsor theatre?" Joanne gasped.

"Quite so." He bowed again. "Now, dear ladies, you will excuse me if I cut this interview short. My feet are shockingly wet and I fear I'm about to catch a chill. I've come to humbly ask lodging for the night, for myself and my man. I will gladly reimburse you whatever it is worth. I simply can't make it to the inn—not in all this weather."

"Of course you may stay here tonight," Joanne quickly replied. "Stay as long as you wish."

"One night will be quite sufficient." His eyes sparkled and his smile broadened.

"You must be hungry from your long journey," Joanne continued. "I'll have Mrs. Sharlock prepare for you."

"That would be most kind of you."

"Will you dine in your room? Or here with me, that is, us?"

He scanned the faces before him. "Why, here with you would be delightful. I'll only be a few minutes."

Joanne rang for Quigg. She gave him instructions and the handsome Mr. Bienville made a lavish exit with a promise of returning momentarily. The three cousins stared at each other and instinctively burst into giggles of anticipation.

CHAPTER SEVEN

Both Alister Tweedly and Toby Albright were summoned to help unload the carriage and ultimately to get the vehicle to the stable where repairs could be made. Mervin Joply, a plain-faced person with unruly brown hair, weak eyes and a peculiar walk, was Matthew Bienville's trusted servant. He was given a room next to his master's in the far east wing where both servant and master could have maximum privacy. The settling in took only a few minutes. Mervin would dine in the kitchen with the cook and retire to the stable to assess the damage done to the vehicle.

When Matthew Bienville returned to the dining room, freshly changed into a stylish brown and beige attire, a ruffled dickey and satin bow, he looked marvelously refreshed and glistening. Brown soft leather boots were on his feet and he carried a substantial linen handkerchief tucked into his lace cuffs. Flat-waisted and grand in manner, he was the picture of cultivated aristocracy. Entering, he kissed the hands of Lydia, Adriane and Joanne. His hold on Joanne's hand lingered longer than with either of the others, his kiss was frighteningly lengthy, and, when his eyes met hers, she felt it impossible to contain her reaction.

"May I have the pleasure of knowing your names?" he asked as he took the place recently prepared for him at the table.

"I am Joanne Phenwick. These ladies are my cousins, Miss Lydia and Miss Adriane Ornby."

"Unless my ear greatly deceives me, I detect non-English accents," he said, smiling mysteriously. "Americans?"

"Yes. How did you guess?" gushed Lydia. "My sister and I are from Portland, Maine, although we had been residing periodically at Greenfield, on the coast of Maine, after our father married a second time."

"I confess I do not know the geography of America. Is Portland, Maine, in the north or in the south?"

The Ornby girls giggled. "It's very much in the north."

"And you, Miss Phenwick?"

"I was born and raised in Boston, Massachusetts."

"I've heard of Boston."

The conversation lingered on mundane topics over dinner. More and more Matthew Bienville's interest became devoted to Joanne at the risk of appearing to avoid the Ornby sisters. However, it was impossible to pull either Lydia or Adriane into an interesting conversation; or if they were included they had nothing to contribute but nervous giggles and foolish reactions.

When supper was complete, Joanne instructed Quigg to light a fire in the library where they would take demitasse and brandy. Neither of the Ornby sisters, who were once again apprehensive of the sound of the storm, were particularly anxious to sit through a conversation from which they would be excluded. Instead, they begged to be excused, amid stifled yawns and sleepy looks.

Privately, Joanne instructed Quigg to remain immediately outside the door to the library, explaining that he was to enter at her slightest call. That arranged, she and Matthew adjourned to the library and waited as the butler served.

Joanne's soft blue skirt was spread about her as she positioned herself on the settee. By then the fire was reaching high and the relatively small room was warm and comfortable. Because of the width of her skirt, Matthew took a chair opposite to her, sitting where the glow of the oil lamp played dramatic shadows over his handsome face. Joanne assumed an informal pose, putting her feet up on the settee beneath her skirt and lounging back in a grand casual manner.

"You must forgive my country cousins," Joanne stated as she observed Quigg retire from the room, catching her eye. "They keep early hours."

"While I am not kindly disposed to country living," Matthew returned, "I understand that rural life inclines to early to retire, early to rise. And often when I am away from London or any other major city for any length of time, I find myself falling into a similar routine. There is so little to do at night, especially when one is single and doxies are not aplenty."

"Doxies?"

Matthew rolled his handsome head back with laughter. "A wrong choice of words. Perhaps a wrong thought. The city is filled with many diversified forms of entertainment during the night hours, one finds much to do.

Here in the country, however, unless one is inclined to reading vast novels, there is little else to do but sleep."

"And conversation?"

"Conversation can become stuffy."

"I'm sorry." She rose dramatically and moved to the fireplace.

"Here, now, I didn't mean present conversation, dear child." He was to his feet and striding toward her.

Joanne turned abruptly and stared into his face. She glanced down all the way to his soft leather shoes, then slowly scanned her way up. "I'm not a child. I don't feel a child any longer, and I don't care to be treated as one."

"Forgive me. I didn't mean to insult you."

"I'm not insulted." She smiled. He returned the smile and something electric happened. She quickly stepped past the man and returned to her position on the settee, spreading her skirts as before.

"You've not had extensive experiences with men, have you?" Matthew commented from the fireplace where he was warming his backside. "Again I don't mean to be offensive."

Joanne swallowed hard. "I've not been raised in a convent, if that's what you're thinking."

"Not in the least."

She turned back to look at him. "I've been acquainted with several young men. At La Chenille, where I went to school, many social events were arranged where young men were invited. There were dances, parties and picnics in the spring and summer. And my Aunt Patricia holds salons with many artistic guests, many of whom are dashing young men. Oh my, yes, really elegant."

Matthew strode toward her as she spoke until he was standing only inches from her. She chattered faster as she forced her eyes into his face. Slowly his head seemed to lower toward hers.

"Aunt Patricia, now that she's a widow, surrounds herself with many handsome men—most of whom are young or at least younger than she is." She turned forward as if to avoid his ever-approaching virile face, turgid lips, hypnotizing eyes. "And Aunt Patricia—Aunt Patricia— well, you would have to know her to understand what I'm talking about." Pushing herself forward, she unwound her legs and reached them to the floor as if she intended to dash away. "Aunt Patricia—Aunt Patricia—" Clear the huskiness. "Aunt Patricia is a poetess."

The large but delicate hands were placed on her shoulders with light forcefulness, gently keeping her from rising. "I should like to meet your Aunt Patricia one day. Is she in England?"

"No. No, in Boston." She tried not to react to his hand softly stroking her neck up and about her ear. Giddy laughter, then immediate attempt at control. "No, Aunt Patricia—well, she presides over society—at least artistic society in Boston. Why are you doing that?"

"Doing what?"

She turned to look at him. Their noses missed touching by a millimeter. Jerking her head slightly back, she could not dismiss the magnetic aura that emanated from him.

"You've never been kissed?"

"Oh—oh, yes," she replied too quickly.

His lips were touching hers and she could not resist. The excitement that she experienced was confusing and beautiful at the same time. A bright flash of lightning startled her, pulling them apart. Wisely Matthew strode toward the window as if intending to pull the draperies.

"No! No, leave them open. I like the lightning, es-

pecially against that window where some of the panes
are stained glass," Joanne said as if she had to find something, anything, to say. Instantly she was on her feet. She
started for the window, then pivoted about and went to
the fireplace. Looking back before she added another
log, she pretended coy indifference.

Matthew stared briefly from the window before he
turned back into the room. "You must forgive me. I don't
wonder you eject me this minute from the house. It is
very rude being so presumptive when hospitality has
been extended. Perhaps I should go—"

"No!" She dashed to the settee and held to the back
of it. "There's no need to go. I'm not offended—not
really—as long as I feel your intentions are honorable."

"Ah, but are they honorable?"

"I took you to be a gentleman."

He flapped his hands to the side and sighed. "Generally I'm a gentleman. But there are times when I
have needs, desires—a longing to be close to someone.
It is easy to forget one's manners at such a time. I suppose it's a reaction from instinct, purely and simply. I
am used to being around theatrical folk, young girls of
no particular moral character who desire to be performers. Most actresses are—well, *eager*."

"I only aspire to be an actress," she replied. "I've not
had the necessary training or exposure. And perhaps it
is only a fantasy I have, a dream. My Uncle Elias was a
minister, we come from a religious family. However,
not to portray us as *the* holy family, we have had our
share of scandal. In fact Uncle Elias shot himself to death
on the altar of the church at which he was head minister.
Scandal was suppressed, and Aunt Patricia played it to
the hilt."

Matthew leaned against the desk, his arms folded.

Eyes penetrated into hers as a knowing smile came to his mouth. "You really are an innocent, aren't you? Oh, I can see your dreams and aspirations written in your face, but, at the risk of offending, I can also see the vast inexperience. Perhaps an apprenticeship in the theatre would change you, inspire your experience and bring out your fullest potentialities."

Another bolt of lightning followed by a rapping at the door. Joanne stared at the window as if she were expecting something or someone to leap in with the next flash of light. Her eyes met Matthew's as the knock came again. Quickly she pushed herself from the back of the settee and sailed toward the door.

Mrs. Sharlock was standing without, her hands folded at her waist, her face a somber, expressionless thing.

Surprised not to see Quigg, Joanne questioned the woman as to why she had interrupted.

"Quigg went to fetch more wood for the fire," Mrs. Sharlock reported. "A caller has come to the door. I refused to permit him enter until Quigg returned. He is wet and muddy."

"Come with me, Mrs. Sharlock, we shall interview him together," Joanne said as she marched fearlessly toward the door.

"Oh, I say," the man said upon recognizing Joanne, "'tis me, Lord Henry Weston. I foolishly went riding before this storm hit. Taking refuge periodically along the way, I thought I could make it on to Falcon Heath Castle, but I see I cannot. My horse is spent, and I, quite frankly, can go no further. I realize Alexander is away, but I thought I might prevail upon your hospitality."

"Fetch a robe, Mrs. Sharlock," Joanne commanded. "And you, Lord Weston, remove your outer garments. By then Quigg will have returned and can help you into dry things. You'll come to the library for hot tea and brandy."

"Delightful, yes, delightful," Lord Henry mumbled. "Would it be too inconvenient for me to spend the night? I'll never make it to Falcon Heath Castle."

Consent was given and Joanne returned to the library, informing that Lord Henry would be joining them in a few moments. The conversation continued along aspects of the theatre as Matthew knew it and his experiences producing dramas for the London stage. Yes, he knew a great many performers, impressarios and the like; and, if Joanne wished, he would introduce her to that element in London.

Lord Henry arrived clad in a robe, a pair of trousers and slippers. A scarf covered his throat and upper chest as he felt a singular tightness which suggested he might be coming down with something. Brandy would help.

In the next hour, it became obvious that Lord Henry and Matthew Bienville were not in accord and argued on several topics from politics and the royalty to opinions of the arts and ultimately of the theatre. Since it was far from being an enlightening experience, Joanne found herself growing bored, hence tired and sleepy. The brandy did little to keep her awake, and the warm fire ultimately had her nodding, catching herself before her chin hit her chest.

The storm continued with sudden vicious gusts of wind and rain blowing against the window panes. Lightning persisted with less and less frequency and seemed to be moving away. Still the electric flashes were apparent.

Joanne rose, moved restlessly about the room, then sauntered toward the window. The men were aware of her, but they were deeply engrossed in argument. She suppressed a yawn as an aching for sleep crept through her.

At the window she watched streaks of water roll down the pane, transparent insects creeping toward oblivion. The glass was cold to her touch and she longed to rest her head against it.

Then she had the sensation that she was being watched, not from the men in the library, but by a pair of eyes outside. Another flash of lightning. No more than ten feet from the house, she saw the person of Jim Cornhill luminated by the eerie glow of jagged light. He was drenched and appeared surprised to be caught by the light and exposed to Joanne's view. She thought she saw him dash toward the side of the building. Still, there was no doubt in her mind that she had recognized Jim Cornhill despite the rain and his wet look, apparel clinging to his muscular body.

She turned to observe the men. "If you gentlemen will excuse me, I believe I will retire for the night. Quigg will be close at hand to attend your needs."

Good nights were expressed and Joanne aristocratically left the room.

CHAPTER EIGHT

Sometime later that night, when Joanne was asleep and Matthew Bienville and Lord Henry Weston had retired to their assigned rooms, a solitary figure crept through the cold halls. His movements were cautious, the only sound he made was nasal—his perpetual sniffles. He carried a candle in a holder, which cast an eerie glow into his pale horse face. His stride was awkward and he periodically lurched forward as if he could not always keep his balance. Large teeth and freckles appeared almost hideous in the candlelight and his upturned nose made his features grotesque. In normal light, he was not all that bad looking.

Stopping at a door, he looked cautiously about before rapping three times, pausing for the count of three, then rapping twice more. He waited a few moments then repeated the coded knocks. Seconds later he heard the bolt being pushed in the door, the key turning and

finally the sound of the door being opened. The candle-
glow shone into Lydia Ornby's face. She had pulled on
a robe and made an attempt at primping her hair.

"Toby?"

"Lydia?"

"Yes," they mutually replied.

"Your sister didn't awaken, did she?"

"I don't believe so."

"Come along then."

"I don't think I should."

"You said yourself that Adriane was a sound sleeper,
didn't you?" Toby Albright stated.

"Yes. But I don't believe I should be roaming around
this old place at night."

"It's not like you would be roaming far, Lydia. Only
down one flight of stairs and into the opposite wing. We
mustn't stand here arguing. Someone is liable to hear
us."

Lydia hesitated a moment before she stepped into the
hallway, pulling the door closed behind her. "I don't
like leaving it unlocked with poor Adriane asleep."

"Everyone has retired for the night."

"But there is a stranger in the house," Lydia whispered. She did not know that Lord Henry was also spending the night.

"The stranger is surely asleep by this time. Come
along. You know we can't have time together during
the day when your sister is awake. She won't let you
out of her shadow. Hurry now."

Toby took Lydia's hand and pulled her forward,
down the corridor to the stairs, to the first floor, across
another corridor and down a hallway leading to the
other wing. En route he warned her not to speak or
make a sound as they would be passing Mrs. Sharlock's

and Quigg's rooms. Beyond the pantry and storage rooms, Toby led Lydia to the chamber he seemed to believe was known solely to him. The door stoutly locked, the candle on the table, Toby said it was safe for them to speak in whispers.

Nearly two hours later Toby walked Lydia back to her room. As the young woman pushed the door ajar, Toby whispered good night and fled into the darkness, finding his way without a candle.

Lydia dreamily entered the room, closed the door behind her, locked it and pushed the bolt in place to make it secure. She fell backward against the door amid romantic speculations. The storm had ceased and moonlight penetrated a crack between the closed draperies. Quickly she went to the bed, removing the pillows she had put in her place. She removed her robe and slippers in darkness and climbed into bed. Feet cold, she wanted to snuggle close to her sister, but restrained herself. Her head on the pillow, she stared at the tiny slit of moonlight coming through the draperies. Romantic speculations. Still she knew that Toby Albright was not the person she could take back to America. Her Grandmother Jane would never approve. She could always remain in England, but how would it look if she were to wed a stableman? So many problems, she thought. If only she could discuss them with her sister. But Adriane did not know that she had even established a rapport with Toby, much less that she found him physically pleasing. Poor Adriane. It was wrong that they were so inseparable; that closeness could direct them to spinsterhood. Adriane with her quiet fear of men. How could Lydia even broach the subject of the stableman to her sister? Adriane would not understand, or would feel betrayed, or become bitter. Adriane . . .

Adriane?

Lydia slowly eased her hand to her sister's side of the bed and felt nothing but bare sheet. Now her hand searched, becoming more and more anxious in its movement.

Finding the pillow empty and the covers pulled back, Lydia jumped to her feet and went to the window where she tore the draperies back. Moonlight flooded, casting its radiance clear to the bed. She could see that nobody was occupying it. Where was Adriane?

A candle lit, then another, Lydia searched about the room. There were few hiding places, none likely. No sign of Adriane. Panic. What should she do?

Three more candles glowed before she sat in the large chair, her robe pulled tightly about her, a blanket over her legs and lap, slippers on her feet.

Did Adriane have a clandestine meeting, too? Had she somehow known of Lydia's rendezvous with Toby, waited for her to leave, then welcomed a friend? No, not Adriane. She had an unnatural fear of men. Besides, her love had been so great for her father, Dr. Johnny Ornby, whom she admired with doting adulation, that another man would never be able to take his place in her life.

Still, perhaps Adriane had been deceptive in her outer attitude toward men, at least to Lydia. Perhaps she had a deep and uncontrollable desire to be with them, but was burdened with Lydia's dependency on her. Nonsense! That just was not Adriane. Lydia would simply have to wait up for her sister. Many speculative thoughts crept into her mind, but were quickly dismissed.

The candles had burned down and out. Lydia had fallen asleep in the chair. The melted wax had turned cold in globs about the candleholders. Dawn lit the

window, then sunlight. While gray clouds were still high
in the sky, rising sun appeared below.

Lydia awakened with a start as a sunbeam fell across
her face. She immediately looked to the bed for Adriane.
Not there. Then she realized that she had locked and
bolted the door when she got back to the room. Suppose
Adriane had come back, found the door impenetrable,
and went to another part of the house to rest and contrive an alibi.

Hurriedly, Lydia dressed herself and left the room.

For the next hour Lydia searched about the old mansion. Members of the household were waking; the servants had been about their duties since shortly after
dawn. Lydia made a point of appearing where she knew
early morning activity would be taking place, asked
seemingly abstract questions and somehow determined
that her sister had not been seen: not in the kitchen,
not by the cleaning and serving people, not by either
Quigg nor Mrs. Sharlock.

Lydia remained in the warm kitchen until she thought
it time for Joanne to be rising. First, she flew to the
room she shared with her sister in some vague hope that
Adriane had returned. Then she checked the rooms in
the immediate vicinity, most of which were not generally in use. Only the chamber which Rebecca had used
looked to have been recently occupied. As she made her
way to the opposite wing, she discovered the empty
room where Matthew Bienville had spent the night. Curiously she examined it as if she thought she might find
a clue to her sister's having been there. Nothing.

Matthew was at the front door with Joanne when
Lydia came downstairs. She remained obscured in the
shadows, close enough to overhear their conversation.

"I will be eternally indebted to you for your hospitality, Joanna," the handsome man recited, taking her hand, bowing low and kissing it. "I hope I may come and call again."

"It would be my pleasure, Mr. Bienville."

"My very good friends call me Matthew."

"Since we have not reached that degree of friendship, Mr. Bienville," Joanne replied, "I shan't indulge in such familiarity."

Mervin Joply arrived at the front door, rapped and informed his master that the carriage was ready. Quick farewells with promises of other meetings, and Matthew was gone.

Joanne reflectively stood for a moment after the door was closed. She was indeed impressed with the man's handsome appearance, with his gallant manners, with his person which she found exciting. Recalling the touch of their lips from the night before, a fire of reaction moved through her again. She felt like dancing and did several gay little steps, a spin about and a leap of enthusiasm. The last of which placed her within a short distance of her cousin.

"Ah, Lydia! What are you doing in such a furtive position?" asked Joanne, attempting to analyze Lydia's enigmatic expression.

"I was just coming down to breakfast," Lydia stammered.

"You've missed the dining room by several degrees, Lydia."

Flustered, Lydia fumbled for further words. "Yes, I know. I was prepared to enter when I heard voices. I came to investigate."

"Where is Adriane?"

"Adriane?"

"I've never known you to appear for breakfast without your sister."

"I thought—that is—you haven't seen her?"

"No."

"Then she still must be in our room," she contrived. "She was restless and must have arisen early. She'll be along any minute."

"Ah, there you are, Miss Phenwick," Lord Henry Weston called as he was about to enter the dining room.

Joanne and Lydia hurried to where he was waiting.

"We were just seeing Mr. Bienville on his way," Joanne said.

"Bienville, eh? Oh, yes. An amazing chap, but not particularly to my liking. Most opinionated," Lord Henry commented. He cleared his throat. "I was looking for a bite of breakfast before I ride on to Falcon Heath Castle. Lady Genevieve will be all in a state with me being away all night. But it couldn't be helped."

"Come in. I'll ring for breakfast immediately, Lord Weston."

The three went into the dining room where a fire was roaring in the fireplace. A cheeriness prevailed.

Lydia sat quietly at the table. She had no appetite, still she pretended to nibble at the food placed before her by the ever-efficient Cyrus Quigg. She only half-heartedly listened to the conversation between her cousin and the noble.

"It isn't wise to open your hospitality to every stranger who comes tapping at your door," Lord Henry remarked. "One never knows what strange individuals may be traveling these days. And look at that poor girl who was found dead in your pasture."

"Not *my* pasture," Joanne corrected. "This house belongs to my Cousin Susannah and Uncle Alexander."

"It would seem that is an odd arrangement," Lord Henry commented. "I should think both Susannah and Lex were your cousins."

"They are. But Uncle Alexander is my father's brother."

"Oh, yes, I never was perfectly clear on that situation. Lady Genevieve attempted to set my thinking straight on that matter, but I'm a bit thick on some subjects."

"Were you familiar with Sara Cornhill?" asked Joanne.

The question caught the round-faced man off guard and he blushed a bright crimson. "No, not hardly. Actually I had seen her about the village. Our neighborhood isn't so large that the residents are unfamiliar. Ira Cornhill, her father, has done odd jobs for me from time to time. Yes, I knew her in that sense."

Joanne realized he was covering the truth with at least an exaggeration if not an out-and-out falsehood. Still she did not challenge his statement. She waited for him to continue his narrative.

"Her death was quite extraordinary. Peculiar circumstances. Oh, I say, speaking of this thing at breakfast doesn't disturb you, does it?"

"Not as long as you do not provide us with gory details," Joanne remarked.

"I don't believe I care to hear any more about such things," Lydia stated. "I've not much of an appetite this morning. Perhaps I should simply excuse myself and see what's keeping Adriane."

Lydia crept from the room and was not missed.

"The curious thing was," Lord Henry continued, "that the flesh of her neck was torn, part missing as if she had been bitten by a vampire."

"A vampire?"

"Well, that was one of the theories. Frankly, I think one of the dogs must have got to her, or perhaps a wild predator of some sort," Lord Henry related. "I believe the verdict is that the crime was committed by a passing stranger who had a bit of a frolic with the girl. Sara was a lass with an eye toward making money. Perhaps she threatened the lad with exposure, or in some other way provoked him. To silence her, he had to dispose of her."

"How dreadful!"

"Still it is only a theory that the murder was a passing stranger held by some of us," Lord Henry added. "Your cousin, that is, your uncle—whatever—Lex is still not beyond suspicion in the matter."

"Uncle Alexander?"

"His memory is a bit cloudy about events of the evening when Sara got herself killed," Lord Henry persisted. "He had been partying a bit. Then he gave a conflicting story: one, that he was here, drinking heavily while he worked in his study; two, that he wasn't even here at the time, but at his apartment in London. When the stories were compared, the conflict was apparent. He said that he had claimed to be in London because he had heard of Jim Cornhill's adamant intention to revenge his sister's death. At any rate it put a mighty suspicious light around Lex. He had to put up a rather large bond with Constable Jones and get special permission to leave for Europe with his wife on her concert tour. Hopefully, it will be over and forgotten by the time they return late next spring."

"Do you think Jim Cornhill will forget if he does not discover the man who—well, who did what he did to Sara?" asked Joanne.

Quigg had come in and served fresh tea. As usual his wig was slightly askew and he appeared to need a shave.

He merely observed, seemingly oblivious to their conversation.

"Admittedly the man is out to seek revenge," Lord Henry commented, "but fortunately he is unaware of Lex's conflicting story. I suspect that Jim Cornhill isn't completely convinced that Lex isn't involved in some way, but he has nothing concrete."

The matter was discussed until after the breakfast things had been cleared. Lord Henry offered further opinion of the type of girl Sara Cornhill was, and he was certain that she was not the angelic creature her father and brother believed her to be. Furthermore her reputation about the village was not secret to many. Even Constable Sedley Jones was fully aware of her ways.

Shortly after, Lord Henry departed, extending an invitation for Joanne and her cousins to come visit at Falcon Heath Castle.

Joanne stood in the cool fresh air, watching as Lord Henry rode out of sight. Then she turned to look at the sky before returning to the house. A shiver went through her, mixed with an ominous sensation.

CHAPTER NINE

Upon entering the mansion, a curious thought struck Joanne. Instead of going back to her own rooms to prepare for the day, she went directly to the chamber occupied by her cousins. Hesitating before knocking, a sixth sense seemed to be warning her that all was not as it should be.

"Yes? Who is it?" Lydia called from within.

"Joanne."

Lydia appeared at the door, opening it a crack. "What is it?"

"Are you all right?"

"Yes, fine."

"And Adriane?"

"She is not feeling herself this morning and is resting."

"Perhaps I should speak to her."

"She's—she's asleep."

"Oh. Then I won't disturb her," Joanne replied. "If there's anything I can do, don't hesitate to call upon me."

Joanne left quietly, moving easily toward her rooms in the opposite wing of the house. Something was definitely wrong. Lydia was not acting herself. Curious thoughts came to her, but she did not want to question Lydia's behavior at that time. She would go to her room, change into warmer clothing and go for a stroll—perhaps a ride.

Lydia remained with her ear to the door. She glanced back at the unoccupied bed. A somber hush fell upon the room. She trembled. Why had she not told Joanne that Adriane was missing? Fear. Fear of exposing the fact that she had left her sister alone in the room while she went off with Toby. Furthermore she would have to admit that she had left the room unlocked when she knew that at least one stranger was in the house.

Toby! She had to go find the stableman to help her search for Adriane. As she changed into a plain woolen outfit, she decided that she would take the back stairs she had taken with Toby hours before and go out the rear of the building and around to the stable. She had no desire to encounter her cousin again until later in the day. By that time, no doubt, Adriane would be found.

A singular urgency seemed to come over Joanne as she changed into warmer attire. She wore woolen undergarments and a loosely fitting skirt over a heavy underskirt. High boots nearly to her knees. A bulky scarf hung loosely beneath her cape. The outfit was nearly too warm for being inside, but she was certain she would need the extra warmth outdoors.

Again before leaving the room, that rush of apprehension came to her. Her hands became so cold she had to go back for a pair of gloves. What was it? Why was she having such feelings? Premonitions? Something definitely was wrong. She scanned the room to see if perchance it was there.

As she descended the stairs, Joanne encountered Quigg. His sudden appearance startled her.

"Oh, Quigg!"

"Excuse me, Miss Phenwick," the man said. He was dressed in outdoor attire himself. A hat covered his head, which he slightly doffed. She could tell that he was not wearing that powdered wig, but she did not get a look at his head without it. "This is the day I must go into London for supplies. I was just preparing to leave."

"To London?" The name conjured magic images in her mind. She had to admit that she liked the excitement of the city. "When will you return?" She was tempted to ask if she might ride along. Perhaps another time.

"By midafternoon or sundown at latest."

"And if it storms again?"

"I will do my best to make it home. Otherwise, I will stay over and return when the weather permits." He smiled patronizingly and excused himself.

Something about his extremely masculine stride, his coarse and unpolished mannerisms appeared attractive to her. What was it? That extreme male image that he projected, the essential animal of the opposite gender? A flood of excitement went through her as she stood and watched until he disappeared from sight. Still her uneasy thoughts about him continued.

Next she encountered stoic-appearing Mrs. Sharlock coming from the dining room. The older woman rarely had much to say, never interested in exchanging small talk. Her grim appearance did not encourage intimacy nor particular confidence.

"Miss Phenwick, I wish a word with you," the house-keeper said, holding herself stiffly erect, hands clenched together at her waist.

"Yes, what is it, Mrs. Sharlock?"

"It is about last night."

"Last night?"

"Late last night. I heards sounds in the corridor outside my room. Whispered voices. Moving footsteps as if some individual or individuals were creeping about. I did not investigate. In fact, I took double precaution to see that my own door was stoutly locked. Still I am certain someone was moving about."

"Did you mention this to Quigg?"

"Yes. But he sleeps soundly and heard nothing."

"What do you suggest be done?"

"That you refrain from permitting strangers to stay in this house," Mrs. Sharlock returned, almost as if she were giving an ultimatum. "After all, you are only a guest here yourself."

Joanne bristled. "I am a Phenwick woman, and Merrihew Manor happens to be Phenwick property. Therefore, Mrs. Sharlock, I am something more than a guest in this house. And, in the future, I will invite whomever I please to enjoy the Phenwick hospitality."

Mrs. Sharlock merely stared. The tight line of her mouth did not alter, but her eyes narrowed as if in a display of annoyance. She turned and walked away without further words.

When Joanne reached the outside, she observed Quigg driving the supply carriage out the front gates. Again she stood and watched and speculated until he was out of sight. Gathering her fantasies, she went to the stable.

Gray clouds did not look particularly threatening, but they could be deceptive. Joanne needed to ride, to exercise, to rid herself of strange notions that were playing in her mind.

Alister Tweedly, despite the coolish weather, was lightly clad in closely fitting attire. His sleeves were rolled up and his blouse was open to expose part of his chest. A broad smile filled his face when he saw Joanne approach. He removed a black knitted cap, and wiped his brow with the back of his wrist.

"Good morning, Miss Phenwick. Going for a ride so early?" He scratched as he spoke. "There are many puddles about and there's chance that there will be more."

"I won't ride far," she replied. "Will you saddle Tommy for me?"

"It will take only a few moments."

Joanne followed him into the stable, unable to avoid noticing how snugly his trousers clung to his backside. Was she having a reaction to every male she encountered that day because of the visit she had had with Matthew Bienville the night before? Had his kiss so inspired her that she wanted to compare his with the lips of other men?

"Funny thing, Miss Phenwick," Alister remarked as he lifted the saddle from its place.

"What is that, Alister Tweedly?"

"Last night, after that man arrived in a carriage," Alister said, "I allowed his man to leave it over there where he could work on it. When Joply, that was his name, went to the kitchen for his victuals, I took a look at the carriage myself. A bolt was missing from the crosspiece all right; but I found the bolt and nut intact on the driver's seat. I think it was purposefully removed."

"Purposefully removed?"

"Ay, to make it appear as if there was mechanical trouble with the rig."

"Perhaps it was merely an extra bolt."

"Ye can believe that if ye like." He laughed and wore a skeptical expression. The saddle was on Tommy. "Toby told me that he awakened early this morning—oh, maybe around two of the clock and said he heard skittering around. He got up and looked out and saw Joply prowling about. There was no mistaking the man's figure since he's nearly bowlegged. Well, a few minutes later he was joined by his master and the two of them went out to the pasture."

"To the pasture?"

"Ay. Toby said to the very spot where Sara Cornhill's body was found," Alister related as he led Tommy toward the door.

"Whatever for?"

"That I could nay tell ye. But Toby said they was actin' mighty suspicious," informed Alister.

A thought struck Joanne. "Alister, will you ride with me?"

"Ride with you?"

"For a short while. I want you to show me the exact place where Sara Cornhill's body was found."

"Ay, I'll do that. But I can walk there and show ye that."

"No. I want you to ride with me, to the pasture and beyond."

Alister slipped into a short jacket, which gave more warmth to his arms than anyplace else, and quickly saddled a gelding called Barney. In an instant he was astride the animal and beside Joanne atop Tommy.

They rode first to the pasture and Alister pointed out

the place where Sara had been found, the area marked out roughly with small stones indicating the position of the body. It was in an open space a distance from any protected places. A large oak tree was nearly fifty yards away. The field was rocky and muddy now.

From there, Joanne indicated she wanted to ride into the woods in the same direction she had gone the day she encountered Jim Cornhill. Many of the trees that were so multicolored on that early ride were now bare of leaves.

Ultimately they reached the spot Joanne believed to be the place where she had met Jim Cornhill. Reining up, she insisted upon dismounting and roaming about. Alister tied the reins to secure the horses and followed her in her quest.

"What is it ye are lookin' for?" asked he.

"I don't know," she confessed. "But I've been here once before."

"By yourself?"

"No. That is, I was by myself when I reached here. Then I met Jim Cornhill."

"Jim Cornhill?" Alister's eyes bulged before he covered his surprise with a nervous chuckle.

Joanne turned to stare fully into the man's face. "Do you know Jim Cornhill well?"

Alister reddened. "Nay, I do not know him well. We've met a time or two. He is one man I do nay care to be too sociable with."

"Why is that?"

"He's not a man to chum around with men friends," Alister informed, "and rarely with the ladies. He's a loner. And I've never put much confidence in men who were loners. There's something strange about them. Besides, Jim Cornhill has a temper when he is upset, or when he gets to drinkin'."

"Is he a hard-drinking man?"

"Nay more than any o' the rest o' us." He laughed. "We all like our ale and our sweets."

"Candy?"

"Nay that kind o' sweets, lass." His eyes had begun to twinkle.

Joanne shivered in reaction to the look he was giving her. He removed his jacket and handed it toward her.

"What's that for?"

"I saw ye tremble."

"I'm not cold."

"Then ye must be anticipatin'."

Her eyes quickly swept over the man before her. She was shocked at her own thoughts. Still she mustered courage to resist temptation. "We'll go now."

"I thought we might have a bit o' a go, lass."

"We will go back to Merrihew Manor, Alister Tweedly. And I want no nonsense from you."

Thwarted, Alister lost his bluster and slumped in submission. "Forgive me, Miss Phenwick. I don't know what came over me."

"You're forgiven, Alister." She handed the jacket back. "We will go now."

As they rode, it was all Joanne could do to keep from thinking what might have happened. She even envisioned how Alister would appear divested of his garments. Such thoughts were not like her. Again she blamed the intimate nearness of Matthew Bienville for her reactions. In that case, she would devote her fantasies to Mr. Bienville and avoid stimulation that might create a natural reaction in Alister Tweedly.

As they approached the mansion and the stable behind it, Joanne caught a glimpse of Lydia running toward the house, obviously from the stable. She urged Tommy faster, dismounted and threw the reins to Alister before he got down from Barney.

CHAPTER TEN

Joanne's first impulse was to chase her cousin. Instead she watched as Lydia disappeared into the building, then she went into the stable to find a motive for Lydia's being there. Alister entered with the horses, taking them to feed and water.

"Who else is in here?" Joanne demanded to know.

"Only Toby Albright stays out here with me," Alister replied while occupied with the horses. "We sleep yonder, but he wouldn't be in there now. Chances are he's gone into the village on errands for cook."

"Into the village? But this is the day that Quigg goes to London for supplies."

"So it is. Still cook may need something what Quigg won't bring back until later. Toby has other chores to do around, tending to the cows and other animals. He could be 'most anywhere."

Toby Albright? Joanne silently questioned. She hardly

knew the man. She recognized him by sight, since he was awkward appearing and not too intelligent. Still she did not know the man or anything about him.

"Where does Toby Albright come from?" she asked as Alister seemed less occupied.

"From th' village. We both do. Not many folk in these parts what don't come from the village, and their parents before them."

Perhaps that was all she needed to know about the person. She glanced about the stable before she picked up her skirts and left. Outside she scanned the country-side in all directions. While it appeared as peaceful as usual, she could not help but sense a kind of tension. The air was static. Was it only because another storm was on the way, or because she was reacting to a pre-monition of some kind? What was it? Why did she have that singular sensation? Gray clouds. Now the sun had been blanketed from view.

She walked several paces away beyond the gate to the stock pen. Chickens clucked and scratched. The geese appeared around the corner of the building and came toward her. She stroked several of their heads before they were replaced with barking dogs. Taking time to pet and fondle, she collected her thoughts. Then, sending the dogs to fetch a stick, she managed to escape into the mansion.

Joanne went first to remove her riding outfit. The heavy boots betrayed her presence in the house. They were left outside her door to be collected by the maid and cleaned. She remained in her woolen underthings, but donned a cotton dress. Green trimmed with light brown. A white shawl about her shoulders. Fires were rarely lit in the house during the daytime, except in a particular room where one might be occupied with handwork or reading.

A short while later, Joanne crossed to the opposite wing of the mansion and went directly to the room in which the Ornby sisters stayed. She tried the door without knocking. It swung open.

"Adriane? Is that you?" Lydia called from a dressing alcove. "Adriane?" She appeared, fastening her dress. "Oh, Joanne."

Joanne was staring at the empty bed. "Where *is* your sister?"

"I—that is—I don't know. She's not here."

"So I see." Joanne stepped toward her cousin. "You've been running. Your face is all flushed and your hair is in need of brushing."

"Running? Why do you say that?" Her face turned suddenly white with pink blotches.

"I saw you."

"Saw me?"

"Running from the stable."

"I was looking for Adriane."

"In the stable?"

"She might have gone to see the horses."

"You told me this morning at breakfast that she was in her room. Was she?"

Lydia did not like to be questioned about the truth. "I said she was."

"Was she gone when you returned from breakfast?"

Lydia thought a moment, turning away and noticing her frightened expression in the mirror. "I think she was."

"She was gone? If she wasn't here you could be certain she was gone."

"I thought she had perhaps gone to breakfast via another route, and I missed her in the process."

"Another route. That would be completely out of her way."

"That is what I thought," Lydia replied. She was trembling.

"Do you know if Adriane had struck an acquaintance with Toby Albright, the stableman?"

"Toby Albright? Adriane?"

"I thought perhaps she might have," Joanne speculated, "since you went to the stable looking for her."

"Toby? Adriane?" She was confused. "No, I didn't go to the stable for any particular reason, Joanne. I had looked about the house for my sister. When I didn't find her, nor Mrs. Sharlock nor none of the servants had seen her, I thought she might have gone for a ride."

Joanne stared at her cousin. She knew she was lying. Breathing deeply, she would not pursue the subject further. A smile. A change of attitude. "I'm going into the village this afternoon if it doesn't storm, Lydia. Would you like to come along with me?"

"Oh, I think not, Joanne. I wouldn't dare leave without —I mean." She turned and began to sniffle.

Joanne went immediately to her cousin, putting comforting hands on her shoulders. "What is it, Lydia?" She turned her about so they were facing.

"Oh, Joanne, I'm worried about Adriane. It isn't like her to disappear like this."

"Shall I help you search?"

"I've been everywhere."

"Perhaps she became moody and, instead of breakfast, she decided to take a stroll. She'll return before long."

Joanne knew her cousins fairly well. Each had confided that the other was restricting to her freedom; they were always concerned about one another. That was a trait their father had placed in them immediately following the death of their mother: they were pledged to look after each other. Hence, they had grown singularly close and dependent upon the other. Joanne had worried that such attitudes would interfere with whatever romantic inclinations they might have. Still, since neither demonstrated any tendencies toward romance other than what they found in novels, she gave it little concern.

By the time she returned to her own room a curious thought struck her. If Adriane were gone—and why did she think that?—then her sister would be free to pursue the course of the courting game. Or perhaps Lydia already had broken away from the strong bond she had with her sister and had developed an alliance with some young man: possibly Toby Albright, or Alister Tweedly, for that matter. They were both rather basic lads with fundamental desires and no particular moral commitment. Had Lydia found her sister away and took advantage of the opportunity for a slight dalliance? She chuckled at the thought. No, that was a bit preposterous. Or was it?

The sun penetrated through the clouds by noon, casting away much of the gloom that had surrounded the morning. Lydia did not appear for the noontime meal, sending word with Mrs. Sharlock that she had developed a headache and wished to remain close to her room. Mrs. Sharlock did not know if Adriane had returned or not.

Joanne could not greatly concern herself with her cousins and their peculiarities. Often she wished they had returned to America with Rebecca. Except, if they had, they might have interfered with Rebecca and Captain Robert Cathcart.

Dressed in a frilly lavender dress, boots, a cape and bonnet and parasol, Joanne informed Mrs. Sharlock that she was going to stroll down to the village. While the parasol was hardly sufficient protection against rain, it was fashionable and could be used for chasing away barking dogs and any other stray animals who found her presence undesirable.

The walk was pleasant and she enjoyed stretching her legs. Her dress was short enough so that it did not drag over the ground, and she often had to lift her skirts slightly as she stepped over puddles.

The village was little more than a settlement of stone buildings clustered about a common grazing plot. A leather shop and tannery, a stable and blacksmith, a tavern, an inn, a supply store which was filled with general merchandise, and a professional building (as it was called), where offices were leased to the constable, an attorney, a physician and other such public servants. In the same professional building was a compartment used as a gaol. The roads were cobbled and sidewalks were designated on each side.

Animals roamed at will, but generally kept their activity to the common. Few vehicles appeared. Cart traffic, usually pushed by hand, was the principal form of transportation. Joanne observed the brief activity before she went into the general store. She was on a looking spree, but if anything caught her eye, she was prepared to buy. The village folk coldly viewed her, aware that she was a Phenwick and an American. They were not well disposed to foreigners, and anyone not native to their village was a foreigner.

Shrewd eyes observed, voices whispered. Children

gawked and were yanked away by cautious mothers. Joanne purchased a small bit of cheese and a crock of honey, which she placed in a cloth totebag. Still the staring eyes, which were becoming annoying and insolent. Whispers, eyes, the combination hurried her from the shop. She had plans of stopping at the bakery, but changed them.

Her shoes made noise over the cobblestones. More curious eyes. Fingers indiscreetly pointing. Now faster. Toward the inn. Approaching the tavern. A pushcart, an old man behind it. She nodded. He ignored her. Then a maid came from the inn who bore remarkable resemblance to her cousin Adriane. Joanne started toward her before she discovered that it was not her cousin.

Adriane? What had become of Adriane? She was the quieter, the least obtrusive of the Ornby girls. Her shy disposition gave her a somber sweetness that only a close relative could appreciate. Her face was egg-shaped with round cheeks, lacking in color and expression. She looked perpetually scared, out of place no matter where the place might be. How dependent she was upon others, especially upon Lydia! Even at La Chenille the Ornby sisters were inseparable until they became a brutal joke to the other girls. Unkind comments often caused Adriane to cry. Red-eyed, she would psychosomatically work herself into an illness and be confined to bed for days with Lydia at her side.

"A cent for your thoughts, lass," a booming voice crashed behind Joanne. A meaty hand went to her waist in a familiar gesture of recognition.

Joanne turned to glare into the unmistakable face of Jim Cornhill. Shocked, she attempted to pull away from the man, but his hold was tenacious. "What is the meaning of this?"

"Come into the tavern with me, and I'll buy ye an ale."

"I don't drink—"

"I'll buy ye a sweet water then," Jim insisted. "Come along. I'll nay molest ye."

Seeing no concerned nor sympathetic eyes in her direction, Joanne allowed herself to be pushed into the smelly tavern. A fire was ablaze at the hearth. Only a few occupants, who observed but made no comment. Jim pushed her toward a shadowed booth and called an order to the tavernkeeper.

"What is it you want of me?" Joanne demanded to know.

"Innermost I want to make wild passionate love to ye," he replied huskily. Then laughter. "Ay, that is me desire, but I'll nay fulfill it lest ye are willin' and as anxious as I am."

"That's comforting to know, since I intend to be neither willing nor anxious," she fired back.

"Other lasses have been of that opinion, too, Miss, have no doubt of that. But opinions are known to change from time to time," he said. The drinks came and he shoved a malignant-looking mug toward her. "Drink. It'll sweeten your temper."

Staring into that remarkably interesting face, she could not avoid the sensuality that exuded from him. Taking him feature by feature, he was not all that well carved; but the combination of ingredients, mixed with the fire of his personality, created an impression that made her react with subtle enthusiasm.

"Why have you brought me here?" she asked, controlling the passions that were rising within.

"I wanted a word with you."

"Then speak that word and let me get on my way."

"Ye saw me last night, didn't ye?" Jim questioned.

"Yes, outside the window in the lightning flash."

"Ay, I knew ye did. I had come lookin'."

"That was apparent."

"Lookin' for the man who killed me sister," he confessed. "I had been asleep since I had put in a hard day of work. I can nay say it was a dream or what it was that awakened me, but something told me to go to Merrihew Manor."

"Go? Why?"

"I don't know. But I had a vision o' me sister, Sara. It was as if she was biddin' me go," Jim stated. "I searched about. Even went to the pasture where Sara had been found. Then I returned to that window where ye saw me and beheld that two men were with ye. The one I recognized was Lord Henry Weston." He spit. "I would nay trust him that far, I wouldn't. He's a fancier of young lasses—very young lasses—but will pursue the older ones when none o' the younger ones are available."

"Why are you telling me all this?"

"Because I want ye to know what I was doing outside Merrihew last night. I did nay want ye to go to the constable and report me. That would only confuse matters and detain me from achievin' what I must do."

"May I go now?" she asked, having taken only one timid drink from the mug.

"If ye wish. But I would rather ye stayed here and kept me company, lass. And perhaps we could go elsewhere to find more privacy, if'n ye be amind."

"I be amind to leaving this instant, Mr. Cornhill," she snapped, fuming at the indelicacy of his suggestion.

"Me name is Jim."

"I am Miss Phenwick and you are Mr. Cornhill, and that's the way it will remain." She rose from the booth.

"If'n ye say so, Joanne!" He slapped his broad hand across her backside. Although muffled by her layers of clothing, it startled her. "Excuse me, Miss Phenwick." He rolled with laughter.

Briskly Joanne left the tavern, emerging into daylight as if she had been catapulted from the room. Straightening her clothing, she hoped she had not been observed. No such luck.

"You will excuse me, Miss," a heavy set man with great wiggly jowls called. Grunting and wheezing as his short legs carried him across the street, he took a moment to gasp for breath, leaning against the side of the building. Bald with a fringe of brown-gray hair gathered in a pigtail at the back of his head, the short round man was a caricature. His attire, while food-splattered and soiled, was of better quality than those worn by the average villager.

"What is it? I'm in a hurry to be on my way."

"And I'm the constable," he managed to say with a belch. "Constable Sedley Jones. I am of the opinion that you are Miss Phenwick, or at least one of the Phenwick relatives."

"I am. Miss Joanne Phenwick, Constable."

"Oh. Then I see why Inspector Stopp was so impressed by you," he remarked. "I had intended to come out and have a look for myself—that is—I mean, I had intended to come out and introduce myself. I'm of the opinion that you three young ladies should not be residing at Merrihew Manor by yourselves without a man about."

"Why so?"

"You've heard of the Cornhill murder, have you not?"

"Yes."

"As long as that crime is unsolved, there is danger

around the old manor," Jones continued. "Even if the Cornhill murder were solved, or even if it hadn't been committed in the first place, I would think it inadvisable for three young ladies to remain there with no man present."

"There are male servants."

"Aha! But male servants are hardly the same thing as a protective male relative or a man of breeding and character to look after things."

"We are managing quite well, Constable." Joanne started to walk away, then turned back. "It was mentioned that Sara Cornhill might have been attacked by a vampire."

"I put no stock in that," Jones replied. "I don't believe in such things—not that my not believing keeps them from existing—but there has never been other evidence of that kind around here. Never any anywhere that has been authenticated. No, Miss Phenwick, wipe the word vampire from your mind."

"Thank you, Constable Jones." She opened her parasol, turned and briskly walked away from the heavy-set man.

Constable Sedley Jones viewed with controlled excitement Joanne's saucy movement as she walked from him. Aware that she was being watched, she impishly exaggerated her swing.

Before she reached the boundary of the business part of the village, a horse and carriage came bolting through. The wheels shook and the clatter was deafening. A short distance ahead the vehicle was brought to an abrupt stop. At first, attempt was made to turn it about, but complicated, it simply waited until Joanne caught up with it. She peered cautiously, holding her parasol low to shield her curiosity.

"Joanna!" the tuneful voice called from the carriage before the door swung open and the handsome figure of Matthew Bienville emerged. "Joanna!"

Joanne repositioned her parasol and accelerated her steps only slightly. "Why, Mr. Bienville. I thought you were gone from my life forever—at least for a few days." She eyed Mervin Joply impatiently sitting on the driver's seat.

"My business was completed in record time," Matthew explained.

"Now you're returning home, wherever home is?"

"My home is presently in London," Matthew said. "I am returning to Merrihew Manor."

"Did you forget something?"

"No." He took her arm and guided her to the carriage. "I left something, however."

"You—"

"My ardent interest . . . my hope. Perhaps a poet might say, I left my heart."

"You left your heart at Merrihew Manor?" A light racing was going on within her, excitement. She knew only too well to what he was eluding. And she was excited merely to be in his presence once again. She accepted the lift up.

"If you say I may," he said as he sat on the seat beside her, "I would very much like to kiss your lips, Joanna."

"My lips?" She nodded, watching as his full lips came toward hers. The touch. The greater excitement and stimulation. Still she had to find control, remember words of wisdom learned at La Chenille: something about not appearing too eager in a man's embrace. Dandy words, but no practical technique was given on how one was to resist the magic plummeting through oneself.

Matthew Bienville, the gentleman, well knew the technique one uses with a lady he finds attractive. He had never been married but he had given much thought to what his approach would be when the ideal person appeared.

"May I stay as a guest at Merrihew Manor for a few days?"

Her throat was hot with excitement so that words were difficult to form. She managed a nod of her head and did her best to gain control of her desires.

CHAPTER ELEVEN

Dark clouds again as the carriage arrived at Merrihew Manor. Joply helped Joanne and Matthew from the
conveyance before he drove it around to the stable.

No more had the striking young couple entered, than
Lydia came flying down the stairs in a terrible state of
mind. She had obviously been crying and was nearly
hysterical. Incoherently, she attempted to explain what
was bothering her. Matthew suggested that they immediately get her to a comfortable room where she could
lie down. Mrs. Sharlock was summoned and a pot of
strong tea ordered.

"Oh, Joanne! Joanne!" Lydia moaned, clinging to her
cousin.

"What is it, dear?"

"Adriane—"

"Has it to do with Adriane?"

Lydia managed to nod her head.

"Adriane has not returned?"

"Not returned?" questioned Matthew. "Where did she go?"

"I don't know," Lydia managed to say before she was convulsed again with tears.

Mrs. Sharlock brought the tea. Joanne instructed the housekeeper to go to the room occupied by the Ornby sisters and see if indeed Adriane was not there.

"I know she's not there," Lydia moaned. "She hasn't been there since last night."

With Joanne holding the distraught girl, Matthew managed to get the tea down her. The warmth somehow had a soothing effect. Lydia seemed to relax momentarily and gain her composure.

"Adriane has been gone since last night?" quizzed Joanne. "But you told she was there this morning."

"I know I did, Joanne, but I wasn't telling the truth."

"But she went to bed with you, didn't she?"

"Yes." A deep sigh, followed by a sob. "My sister fell almost immediately to sleep, as she usually does. But I had difficulty putting certain thoughts from my mind. I couldn't sleep." Her eyes darted about like a discontent moth. She was contriving a tale and she wanted to be certain to remember all that she said. "I was tossing so fitfully, that I decided to get up lest I disturb Adriane. When I still did not feel drowsy after some time of pacing the room, sitting in the chair and pacing again, I believed that milk might perhaps calm my nerves. I went to the kitchen were I found a pail of milk on the drainboard. I took a glass, then returned to the room. When I reached the chamber, I was surprised to find that Adriane was not there. I looked about. Then went to the room again. Still not there. I became alarmed. Fear moved me and I locked and bolted the door. I sat in the chair to await her return. But I fell asleep. No doubt Adriane returned and found the door locked. For some reason she didn't try to awaken me."

"*If* she returned," Matthew said.

"But she must have returned and found the door locked."

By then Mrs. Sharlock appeared with news that Adriane indeed was not in her room. At which, Joanne insisted that all the servants, everyone at Merrihew Manor, be assembled and be given instructions to search for the missing girl.

When brought together, Joanne explained to the staff what had happened and advised them to make a thorough search of the premises.

Toby had listened to the story. He realized that Lydia had constructed it as she had to protect him, or not to arouse suspicion about their having been together the night before. Volunteering to search the nether regions of the mansion, he managed to give Lydia a knowing glance in parting.

Alister Tweedly took Mervin Joply with him to go over the stable and the grounds in the near vicinity. Rain had begun, presenting a problem in extensive outdoor searching.

Nearly an hour later the staff reported back that no trace of Adriane was to be found in any section of the house. Lydia became nearly hysterical, wailing and frantically calling for Adriane. Matthew actually had to catch her in his arms when she ran from the downstairs parlor. Finally it was decided that Quigg, who had arrived home from London, should go immediately for Dr. Ebenezer Cummings, the local physician.

While waiting for Dr. Cummings to arrive, Joanne and Matthew, with the aid of Mrs. Sharlock, managed to get

Lydia to her room. However, the thought of remaining in that room without her sister sent the young woman into frantic crying. Another room was prepared for her. Eventually Mrs. Sharlock and Joanne got her ready for bed in time for the doctor's appearance. Mrs. Sharlock remained to assist where she could.

"I do not understand what all the uproar is, Miss Phenwick," commented Quigg as Joanne descended the stairs in the company of Matthew Bienville.

"The problem is that Adriane, my cousin, disappeared during the night and has not returned," Joanne said simply.

"Ah . . . perhaps . . ." Quigg remarked mysteriously.

"Yes. What is it?"

"I was awakened in the wee hours," the butler informed. "I believe a dog was barking or some other animal was creating a havoc. I do not awaken rapidly, hence remained a bit groggy for several minutes. When I had completely gained my senses, whatever sound that had awakened me was quiet. I rose from bed for a functional purpose, knocking my toe in the process against the bedpost. Then, limping with pain, I occasioned to go to the window to see if the storm was still persisting. Rain had ceased and the moon was clear in the sky. I was about to return to my bed when I saw the figure of a woman clad in a white nightgown with a light shawl about her shoulders. She looked to be sleep-walking, going out toward the front gate. I fumbled for a match, again banging my foot, which caused me to yelp through a song and dance before the pain eased. Candle lit and pulling into my breeches, I hobbled back to the window to note that the woman was no longer in view—but there was a man: a large bulky man. I would appear small beside him."

"Did you get a close look at the man?" asked Joanne.

"He came within perhaps fifty meters of the house," Quigg related, "and the moonlight once caught him in the face. But it was too great a distance in that light to determine who it might be. The man quickly disappeared into the shadows. Because my foot was still throbbing, I stood by the window to watch for further activity. I saw none."

"Could you tell if the woman was my Cousin Adriane?"

"No, Miss Phenwick," Quigg responded, "I would be telling a falsehood if I were to say that. For, although her hair appeared dark, it could have been any shade from my point of view."

"Have you ever had occasion to speak with Miss Ornby, Quigg?" questioned Matthew.

"I do not understand the question, sir."

"I was simply trying to establish your familiarity with the young lady," Matthew explained, "that is, if you had had contact enough with her to be able to recognize her —say if she were ten meters away."

"Oh, yes, I knew her appearance, sir," Quigg replied. "She was no raving beauty. You will forgive the observation, Miss Phenwick, but I am a person with eyes, and I did take notice of her. A man of menial servitude such as I does not have the choice of female creatures—again you'll pardon the reference, Miss- -that those of higher station are permitted."

Joanne suppressed a smile. Quigg's humility somehow appeared exaggerated, for she was certain that such a man, despite his position in life, had a tremendous appeal for women. She herself had concluded that he was no doubt the best-looking male at Merrihew Manor.

"In other words you feel certain that you would have definitely recognized Adriane Ornby if she had been close enough and the light was sufficient?" said Matthew.

"Yes, sir."

"And you could not honestly say the lady you saw was Miss Ornby?"

"In all honesty, no, sir." Quigg glanced about. "If you've no further questions, I would like to get on with me work. I've got the carriage to unload and things to put away. And the rain *is* coming down."

"One last question, Quigg. Are you familiar with the man known as Jim Cornhill?" Joanne inquired.

"Jim Cornhill, Miss?" Quigg's face became a blank, his brown distant eyes blinked as if repeating the question. "Although I have been in employ at Merrihew Manor for many years, I have never made an effort to become acquainted with the villagers." Disdain in his voice. "I barely know many of those who come to work here unless they are hired for an extended period of time."

"Then you have never heard the name before, Quigg?"

"That is not true, Miss Phenwick," he replied, now a bit more animation in his face. "I have heard the name. Sara Cornhill was the name of the lass who was murdered and her body found in the pasture. Her father is Ira Cornhill, her brother is Jim. I have spoken with the father on one occasion prior to Mr. Phenwick granting him an interview. I must say I was not favorably impressed with the old man. Is that all, Miss?"

"Yes, you may be excused, Quigg."

Quigg moved away with a firm stride. Agile. Proud. Determined. Sturdy back. Legs of an athlete bulged obviously through his tight silk hose and the snug-fitting breeches.

"What do you make of that?" questioned Matthew.

"I don't know. Of one thing I'm certain and that is that

I am terribly cold," Joanne commented with a shiver. "Can't we go somewhere that is warm?"

"All of the rooms should have wood laid for fires by now," Matthew said. "Take your pick of rooms, and I'll see that you have a roaring fire in a matter of minutes."

"There is a sitting room in my suite," she suggested. "And I know for a fact that wood is on the hearth."

Matthew knelt before the small fireplace, small in comparison with some of the others in the house, which were large enough for a man to stand inside without ducking his head. Crackling sounds as the fire gripped the logs and blazed upward.

Joanne got a heavy robe and wrapped it about her shoulders, still shivering. She got as close to the fire as she dared.

Matthew, when he turned back from observing his work, went to her, noticing her trembling.

"Here. Allow me," Matthew said as he reached around her, stepping as close as he could to generate some of his heat to her.

Magnetic energy exuded from the man and Joanne could not help but be drawn closer to him. What she felt was more than a physical reaction. Her emotions were affected, although she did not analyze precisely what was happening. Never had she experienced such a sensation in the presence of any other man, nor had she dreamed that such was possible. Warmth came to every part of her body at once and she felt her face glistening with a heated glow. Their eyes were fixed on each other's; the softness of breath touched the other's face; the lips came so close that neither could resist the other's lips. More excitement! Greater warmth! Something exploding within the innermost part of each of them. Turgid lips meeting soft lips; weathered and lightly whis-

kered skin caressing smooth and creamlike skin.
Feminine strength meeting masculine strength and ac-
quiescing to the sheer wonder of it. Then the gentle
kiss, the light caressing, the slow easing of pressure until air once again moved through that space between
them.

"I had no choice but return to Merrihew Manor," Matthew said, "if only to taste again of this. Yet when I left
this morning, I was disappointed and in need of easing
my annoyance with one of the street girls in London. Still
I could not." He stepped away from her, taking a moment
to survey the room. "A new fascination had come over
me. I had touched perfection, and anything less would
only be disillusioning." Again he faced her, this time
with several paces between them. "I did not return to
take advantage, to woo you with pretty phrases for the
purpose of getting my way. No, on the contrary. I came
back to get to know you better. You, the mind and soul
in that gorgeous physical creation. Touch. Yes, I must
touch, lightly caress, feel the reality of divine communi-
cation. But never with disrespect nor dishonor."

"In that case," she whispered, "perhaps I should
apologize for my thoughts." Swallowing hard, she turned
back to watch the leaping flames. "I admire your candor,
Matthew. It makes me want to trust you fully, without
reservation."

Four steps and he was beside her again. Arms about
her waist as he stood behind. "That faith and confidence
is what I need most."

Matthew had moved the settee so that it was facing
the fireplace. There they sat, his arm about her; her
arm gently resting over his leg.

"I'm tired of wandering, Joanna," Matthew confessed in
the course of their time together. "I desire to settle

down. I'm a good businessman. And, because of my experience in the import trade, I have long thought I might like to be involved with Medallion Enterprizes. Quite frankly, I did not have carriage trouble last night. I had Joply remove a crucial bolt to make it appear so."

"For what reason?"

"I didn't realize your uncle was away," Matthew explained. "It was a contrivance in hopes of getting the opportunity to speak with Mr. Phenwick. Whereas I didn't achieve that aim, I stumbled on to something more exciting and stimulating."

"Perhaps I can exert some influence in your behalf," Joanne said. "After all, my father is head of the Boston branch of Medallion, and Uncle Alexander is my father's brother."

"If you could, I would be most appreciative," Matthew returned. "But I don't want you to get the impression that what you can do for me as far as Medallion is concerned has any bearing upon our personal relationship."

Joanne smiled sweetly, looking directly into his face. Then she closed her eyes, cocked her head slightly and waited for his kiss.

CHAPTER TWELVE

The next day was sunny with only traces of clouds in the sky. An early search was made throughout the mansion for Adriane. Still no trace of the girl. Her clothing was examined. None of her dresses were missing, only the nightclothes she wore the night of her disappearance.

Matthew decided to do a bit of investigating on his own; hence he left by midmornig with Joply and drove into London. He had further personal business to which he had to attend as well.

Less than an hour after Matthew left, Quigg appeared to Joanne in her sitting room, to announce that she had a caller: Mr. R. Piedmont Stopp. Joanne sent word for the Scotland Yard inspector to wait in the library for her. Quigg was instructed to light a fire since, despite the sun, there was autumn chill in the air.

Five minutes later Joanne appeared at the library

door, where a fire was just beginning to blaze. R. Piedmont Stopp was staring out the window when she arrived and turned abruptly for her entrance.

"Good morning, Inspector Stopp. I wasn't quite expecting you this morning," she said grandly as if she were the mistress of the house.

"Lovely morning, kind lady, with the exception of seasonal cold." He twitched his moustaches with the movement of his lip. "I have a room in the inn and have been using the opportunity to scout about. It was while I was bending my ear to local conversation that I overheard the rumor that your cousin is missing. Is it true?"

"I'm afraid it is. She just seems to have disappeared. We've looked everywhere," Joanne confided. "Had I known you were so close at hand, I would have made a point of calling upon you first thing this morning."

"Ah, then it is lucky that I have come along when I did."

"May I offer you something?"

"Only a seat, dear lady. My legs are a bit weary from a great amount of hiking about yesterday."

"A great amount of hiking?"

"About the village, around to the farms and through the forests," he explained. A gust of air emptied from his lungs as he sat. "I was merely making the rounds, you might say, getting the complexion of the land. Lovely country up here, rustic and rural."

"You heard that Adriane was missing?" Joanne asked, taking a seat opposite the man.

"Yes, only this morning while having breakfast at the inn," he answered. "Some fish-faced creature who was waiting tables had mentioned it to another of the oafs who is employed there. I beckoned him to my table and extracted the information from him. He, of course, had never seen your cousin."

"How did that person know about Adriane? That is a mystery."

"Word travels fast in a small village like this. Your household staff was sent to search for the missing girl, were they not?"

"Yes."

"'Tis simple to follow the trail from there." Stopp leaned back and stroked his girth. "Your scullery told the scullery down the street, who was a girlhood friend. Like wildfire the word is spread—perhaps not accurately, but well."

Joanne then told him all she could about the disappearance of Adriane Ornby.

"I should like to have a word or two with the missing girl's sister, if I might," said Inspector Stopp.

"Lydia was upset yesterday over the disappearance of Adriane," Joanne related. "And she did not come down to breakfast this morning. The housekeeper looked in on her a short while ago and she was still asleep. The doctor was called last night and he gave her powders."

"Nonetheless I should like to interview the girl if it is humanly possible," Stopp declared, pushing himself to his feet.

The stairs left the large detective slightly winded, still he gathered his wind by the time he reached the room in which Lydia was staying.

"Shall I wait outside?" Joanne asked.

"No, I would prefer you come in with me," the inspector said, "and do your best to assure her that I am only inquiring about her good."

Lydia was awake and had been for nearly forty-five

minutes. Still she closed her eyes upon hearing the knob turn. She pretended to be breathing deeply in sleep.

"Lydia? Wake up, Lydia. Joanne here. I must speak with you. It's about Adriane."

Lydia blinked her eyes open and looked pathetic before she saw R. Piedmont Stopp, then she appeared frightened. "Has—has Adriane returned?"

"No." Joanne went closer to the bed. "Lydia, this is Inspector Stopp from Scotland Yard."

"You didn't have to go to Scotland Yard. I'm certain Adriane will turn up," Lydia moaned, unable to hide her apprehension.

"Ah, yes, I recall meeting you the night of Lord and Lady Smilington's party for your other cousin, the pianist," Stopp exclaimed as he neared the bed. "My memory is dim at times. I did not quite recall which name went with which sister. So you're Lydia. Now I recall Adriane. Ah, but you must be famished, my dear child, you haven't had breakfast. Perhaps we should come back once you've had some nourishment."

"I'm not much hungry, thank you," Lydia said weakly.

"A glass of milk perhaps?" Stopp suggested.

"No, I'm not much partial to milk, it curdles in my—" She caught herself. "I mean . . ."

"Yes, Miss Ornby, you were saying?"

"I forget."

"It was about milk curdling in your digestive area, I believe."

Lydia turned to her cousin. "Joanne, why have you brought this man here? What is he doing in my bedroom?"

"He must speak with you, Lydia. He is only inquiring about your good."

Stopp blinked and formed a fatherly smile. "Quite so,

my child. I am concerned, however, that if you have such a negative reaction from drinking milk, why you would make your way down to a dark kitchen for a cup of milk in the middle of the night. Certainly if it curdles once inside you, it would hardly seem the thing to soothe your distraught nerves. Now, isn't that so, dear child?"

Lydia looked down. "Yes."

"For what purpose then, did you leave your room the night before last?" Stopp persisted.

Now terrified, she stared at the man, then looked quickly to her cousin and back. "I—I—I don't know."

"Lydia, you must tell Inspector Stopp why you left your room that night. He only wants to help," Joanne urged.

Lydia whimpered. A scared animal, she wanted to hide beneath the covers.

"Could it be that someone came to your door to get you?" Stopp persisted. "Perhaps a gentleman caller."

"Oh, Inspector Stopp, I don't think—" Joanne interrupted. "Lydia isn't familiar with any—I mean, who could have possibly—"

"Miss Ornby has been at Merrihew Manor for sometime now, as you have been, Miss Phenwick," Stopp continued. "Time enough to establish some sort of alliance—perhaps with one of the staff."

"What are you suggesting, Inspector Stopp?" Joanne exclaimed.

"I don't mean to be offensive, Miss Phenwick," he said, "but I am familiar with human nature and there are certain things which cannot be denied. If you think it not possible, I suggest that you not underestimate the desirability of Miss Ornby. I personally find her not unattractive."

Lydia fell for the Inspector's ploy. "That's true, Joanne, you've always underestimated me because you're so pretty and I'm rather plain. But I have had experience."

"You have had experience?" question Joanne incredulously. "With a man?"

"Don't look at me like that!" Lydia shrieked defiantly. "Why should I have not had such an experience? I am a human being, too. I have feelings and desires." Her hands flew out as if she were attempting to scratch at Joanne. "I do not want to be stuck my entire life an old maid with Adriane my only company and source of companionship! Perhaps my name is Ornby, but I am a Phenwick woman like the rest of you."

"Of course you're a Phenwick woman, Lydia," Joanne tried to console.

Coldly Stopp sat on the bed, separating the two girls. He gazed intently into Lydia's eyes. "Did you have anything directly to do with your sister's disappearance?"

"Not intentionally," Lydia murmured. "But indirectly I must have had, because I left her alone and went out of the room without locking the door."

"And when you left the room," Piedmont pounded, "where precisely did you go?"

"Down the back stairs, through the servants' quarters and beyond to a distant chamber," Lydia hesitantly reported.

"A distant chamber on the first floor?"

"Yes, I believe it was."

"Now this person who came to your room—who was he?" asked Stopp.

"I cannot tell you. I would not want him to get into trouble," Lydia whimpered.

"Even if he were in some way responsible for the disappearance of your sister?"

"He wouldn't—at least I don't think—" She cast a feeble glance at Joanne. "I don't feel his identity should be known to Joanne."

"Then will you tell me alone?" Stopp asked.

"Only if you swear you will tell no one else."

"If he is not part of a convoluted plot," Stopp returned, "I swear to keep his identity a secret." He turned to Joanne. "If you please, Miss Phenwick. This is the only way we will get anywhere in this matter. Will you wait outside for me?"

Joanne could barely believe her ears. The entire disclosure had come as a shock. Lydia involved in an illicit affair was more than she could fathom. She nodded and silently left the room.

While waiting in the hallway, a list of men went through Joanne's mind. Yet there were two guests in the house that night as well as the regular staff. She was certain neither Matthew Bienville nor Lord Henry Weston would have been involved—at least not with Lydia. Adriane? No, she refused to speculate further until she had a chance to speak with Piedmont Stopp.

When the inspector left Lydia's room, he was as confounded as he had been earlier. He scratched his head thoughtfully, then caressed his moustaches with the side of his index finger.

"Did she tell you?"

"How's that? Oh, yes, quite," Stopp responded. "I'm pledged to secrecy. I hardly suspect a conspiracy in the matter. Just a bit of carelessly leaving the bedroom door unlocked, I suspect. If they will, I would encourage both Misses Ornby to leave Merrihew Manor at the earliest opportunity. I further suggest that they return to America."

"Return? That is, of course, if Adriane is found."

"If she is not, or if something critical has happened to her," Stopp commented as they walked down the hallway, "I would insist that Miss Lydia go back to America by herself."

"And the man?"

"I will see if I can't have a chat with him and discern anything further from him," Stopp said. "But my suspicions are that Miss Ornby and her friend were having a somewhat innocent bit of sport with no malice intended."

As they reached the head of the main stairs, Quigg appeared at the foot of them to announce that Constable Sedley Jones had arrived and was waiting in the library.

"My dear Miss Phenwick," Stopp stated, mustering his most courtly style, "would you be so kind as to entertain Constable Jones for fifteen or twenty minutes. I prefer to conduct an interview or two without his able assistance —if you know what I mean."

Joanne sighed. "I'll do my best."

Joanne went to the library where the short, stocky man was waiting, while Piedmont Stopp went to the stable.

"Constable Jones, it's pleasant to see you again." She was lovely and he was intrigued.

"Miss Phenwick."

"I know you came to speak with Inspector Stopp," she said. "He will be with you anon. Won't you have a seat? Perhaps you would care for a drink. A cup of tea, perhaps?"

"Yes, tea would be fine."

Joanne rang for Quigg and turned back to observe him scanning the interior of the library. She watched him a moment before he realized what she was doing.

Reddening, a nervous chuckle gurgled in his throat.

"I've not often been in Merrihew Manor. While your relatives entertain occasionally, most of their guests come from London or, I suspect, from abroad. I admit I have come within listening distance of Mrs. Phenwick when she was practicing for a concert. In the summer she leaves the windows open in the music room and from that large oak out there, one can get quite an earful of the glorious strains of her playing."

"I had no idea that you were interested in music."

"I appreciate hearing melodies that are played as grandly as Mrs. Phenwick executes them," Sedley Jones explained. "I have been known to drive into London for one reason or other, and while there, take in a concert or two."

Quigg arrived with the tea and announced that Joanne had another caller.

"Another?"

"Lord Henry Weston."

"Don't tell me he left his sock and came to reclaim it," Joanne remarked sarcastically.

"I don't believe he left a thing, Miss," replied Quigg in his usual officious way, taking himself seriously. "He did not state his business."

"Show him in here, please." Joanne waited until Quigg left the room. "I wonder what this is all about. You know Lord Weston, don't you, Constable?"

"I should say I do," the portly man replied. "I have often been invited socially to Falcon Heath Castle. Lady Genevieve and I have a little project we've been collaborating on: an historical project, gathering data about this area—particularly Falcon Heath Castle—to be recorded historically." A smile of satisfaction.

"I had no idea."

Lord Weston, complete in stylish riding attire, came

bounding in as if he had only two minutes to spare. Glancing back at Quigg, he took the liberty of closing the door in the butler's face.

"That man gives me the shivers," Lord Weston stated. "All butlers give me the shivers. It's their attitude. I suppose I was terrified by one as a wee lad and it's carried over into my adult life." In a little skipping movement, he managed to reach Joanne with outstretched hand. "Ah, my dear Miss Phenwick! You must forgive my flustered entrance, but I've been riding rather rapidly and am still a bit joggled up inside. Ah, you here, too, Jones? Fancy that. Well, well. I stopped by the inn to call upon Piedmont Stopp and was informed that he had come here. I expected to see the inspector, not the constable."

"Likewise," Jones commented, "I expected to see the inspector and not—well, not anyone else."

"Fancy that," Lord Weston snorted and looked longingly at the tea things.

"Oh. May I offer you a cup of tea? I was just preparing to pour," Joanne said, enjoying the byplay between the two men.

"I say, that would be pleasant," Lord Weston returned.

As she presented the tea cups to the men, Joanne chatted. "Constable Jones was just telling me about himself and your wife—"

Lord Weston rattled his cup in the saucer. "The cad!"

"No, no," Jones returned. "I was merely relating about the historical project Lady Genevieve and I have going."

"Hysterical project, if you ask me!" Lord Weston fired back. "Genevieve is notorious for her hanky-panky, whatever she may call it."

"And your little erotic adventures go unnoticed?" Jones retaliated. "Why, they verge on scandal."

"Hush! Good Lord, man! Have you no decency? No sense of respect for this young lady's unsullied ears?"

"Then you shouldn't have insinuated about Lady Genevieve—"

"Nonsense! It's true!"

"Gentlemen, please!" Joanne interrupted. "Perhaps I should excuse myself and let you continue your conversation in private."

"I've no desire to continue this conversation," Lord Weston grunted. "I came here for the purpose of seeing Piedmont Stopp, and that alone. I'll not permit myself to be flustered by this—this—constable."

The men finished their tea in silence while Joanne amusedly looked from one to the other, expecting either or both of them to begin firing again momentarily.

Finally when Lord Weston could no longer tolerate the annoying silence, he set his tea cup down and stood abruptly. "I shall go search for Inspector Stopp."

"I was about to suggest that I would do the same thing," Jones remarked.

"If you go, I shan't. And I was the first to announce my intentions."

"Unless you knock me cold on my arse, you'll not leave this room first."

"Are you threatening me, Jones?"

"Gentlemen, please!" Joanne rose and stepped bebetween them. "I suspect that Inspector Stopp was going toward the kitchen to speak with the household staff. Chances are he is there, or out toward the stable, or beyond. The lads are working in the fields today, salvaging what was not ruined by the rains. Why don't we three stroll in that direction and see if we can't find the inspector?"

"Very well," Lord Weston said, "but when we find him, I shall speak my piece first."

Jones shrugged. He was not inclined to continue the argument.

Inspector Piedmont Stopp had indeed been in the kitchen chatting with the household staff, the live-in servants and the day-laborers who came from the village. They had all heard of the disappearance of Miss Ornby, but none had information about her. He was barraged with opinions about Sara Cornhill, however, until he practically ran from them.

In the stable, Piedmont had found the room occupied by Alister Tweedly and Toby Albright. Neither man was present. He discovered nothing of particular importance since each man had few possessions. While there, however, Toby arrived. The large inspector confronted the stableman with the information he had about himself and Lydia Ornby. At first Toby denied knowing anything about it, then confessed that what he said was true. To him it was only a bit of fun because Miss Ornby had encouraged it so. Stopp appeared to believe the man and did not detain him longer.

Outside, Stopp stretched as he sniffed the fresh air mixed with the scent of animals. A chill autumn breeze. The sun had disappeared behind gray clouds. The geese were running in the distance, going toward the front gate. He considered himself lucky, and thought it prudent he leave the immediate vicinity as quickly as possible.

As he started toward the mansion, he was distracted by distant barking of dogs. Beyond the stable, away from the house, two hounds were suspiciously crouched front down in the pasture. He was about to go investigate, when Joanne arrived with Lord Henry Weston and Con-

stable Sedley Jones at her heels. Each of the men were
puffing since she moved swiftly, not unlike a dancer.
Jones especially was red and gasping for wind when
they reached Stopp.

Both men tried to speak at once, but all that came
forth was a chorus of grunts, wheezes and gasped sylla-
bles. Joanne smiled and winked good-humoredly at Piedmont Stopp. The entire matter had struck her as so
humorous that she could barely keep from rolling with
uncontrolled laughter. Stopp suspected this, and twinkled his eyes in reaction.

"While you two are regaining your composure," Stopp
declared, "I'll go out to the pasture and have a look at
what is fascinating those dogs."

"We'll come, too," Lord Henry managed to announce,
meaning himself and Joanne.

Constable Jones simply pointed at himself, indicating
that he did not intend to remain behind.

Stopp and Joanne took long strides over the field, side-
stepping puddles and muddy places as best they could.
Lord Henry was five paces behind them, and the constable was a good ten.

The inspector stopped suddenly, shielding his eyes.
"Good Lord!" he uttered. "Do you know those dogs?"

"Jaspar and Alonzo, I believe."

"Will they come to you?"

"They usually do."

"Call them. Get them away from that place. Take
them back to the house with you."

"I don't understand."

"What is it?" Lord Henry asked. "My heavens! Isn't
that the spot—"

"Precisely the spot on which Sara Cornhill's body was

found," Stopp assured him. "Call the dogs away, Miss Phenwick."

Joanne called the dogs, but they were too preoccupied to respond. Impulsively she ran ahead with Inspector Stopp directly behind her. Fortunately the dogs wore rope collars, by which she was able to grab them. Then she saw the body and, still holding securely to the animals, she screamed.

"Constable," Stopp ordered, "get her out of here!"

"No. Let me remain," Joanne stated as she stared incredulously at the sprawled body in the confines of the stone image that outlined the exact position in which Sara Cornhill was discovered.

The dogs were barking furiously as Inspector Stopp crouched to examine. He turned the head with the staring eyes slightly to the side; then glanced up at Joanne. No doubt in her mind, she nodded and felt as if she were going to be sick.

"No doubt in your mind that this is your cousin?" Inspector Stopp put the question in words.

Joanne looked away. Tears. Emptiness and yet a stabbing in the pit of her stomach. What she had feared but refused to express, had happened.

Lord Henry Weston stepped forward. "I recognize the girl. That is most definitely Miss Adriane Ornby."

Joanne heard no more of the men's conversation as she slowly tugged the dogs away from the dreadful sight.

Alister Tweedly was at the stable. He saw her coming and having difficulty with the dogs who wanted to return to the pasture. The tall groom ran forward and took the dogs from her.

"What's the excitement out there?"

"Please help me to the house at once, Alister, I feel faint."

Toby came running. He accepted the hounds from the groom and guided them to the stable. Alister put his arms about Joanne and lifted her. In his strong hold, next to his handsome person, she sagged and seemed to collapse as he hurriedly carried her to the mansion.

CHAPTER THIRTEEN

The wizened old Dr. Ebenezer Cummings was summoned to examine the body and fill out a certificate of death. Once that was accomplished, and it was his opinion that strangulation was the cause of Adriane's demise, the wobbly man with pure white hair went to examine both Lydia and Joanne. It was while in the company of Dr. Cummings that R. Piedmont Stopp and Lord Henry Weston informed the girl of her sister's murder. At first a squeal of shock, then Lydia seemed to become immobile, silent, and accepted the announcement as if she had already prepared herself for that inevitable fate.

Dr. Cummings gave her something to soothe and promote sleep. He was of the opinion that sleep was the best medicine for shock. Lydia reluctantly took the potion, making a face as she swallowed it. Then she scanned the expressions observing her. Constable Sedley Jones had recently squeezed his way into the room and peered about Lord Weston with an expression of impish curiosity.

"What is to become of Adriane?" asked Lydia.

"I should think that would be your decision," Lord Weston commented. "Do you wish to take her back to America with you?"

"I had thought we both would be buried in the Phenwick cemetery at Greenfield where my father is. But I think it would be best to arrange a simple ceremony in the Merrihew chapel and have her buried here with her distant ancestors." She yawned. "And what is to happen to me?"

"My dear, I insist that you leave this place instantly and come stay at Falcon Heath Castle while you recover from your grief," Lord Henry suggested.

"But what of Joanne?" the girl asked, now showing distinct signs of drowsiness.

"I shall invite her to come to Falcon Heath, too," Lord Henry replied. "We have ample room. And Lady Genevieve thrives on having guests stay for extended periods of time. Poor old girl gets a bit lonely, I should surmise."

"I would be pleased to go to Falcon—Falcon Heath," Lydia sighed, "whether Joanne goes or not." Her eyes closed, then came open again. "Please . . . I would prefer that Adriane be buried no later than tomorrow." The eyelids shut again and she breathed deeply.

The men tiptoed from the room. Mrs. Sharlock was instructed to keep watch over Lydia, or arrange for another of the older women in the house to sit by her. She was not to be disturbed until the next day in time for funeral arrangements.

"But should she spend another night at Merrihew?" questioned Lord Henry as they descended the stairs.

"She must not be moved in her present state," Dr. Cummings insisted.

They were joined by R. Piedmont Stopp, who had been with Joanne. He informed them that she was simply being emotional at such a time of shock and sorrow, but that he had faith she would be quite all right shortly.

In the library, where Quigg served brandy as ordered by Lord Henry, the four men sat about as if they were at a men's club, detachedly discussing the matters of the day. Quigg, while not displaying any outer emotion, inwardly scowled at their presumptuous informality as he built a fire. The servant, after ascertaining that nothing more was wanted of him, was about to leave the room.

"Oh, Quigg, there is one thing," Piedmont Stopp interjected, catching the man at the door.

"Yes, sir?"

"You were away most of the day, weren't you?"

"Yes, sir, that is correct."

"And when you returned back to Merrihew Manor?"

"There was confusion and I had a task or two to which I had to attend. Then the unloading of the carriage had to be superintended. I have had an extremely busy day."

"In conversation with Miss Phenwick, she mentioned that you had been awakened the night before last and had seen the figure of a young lady," Piedmont said, "and that of a bulky man outside a distance from your window."

"That is true," Quigg replied, and related the story that he had earlier told to Joanne and Matthew.

"Were you ever in a position today," Piedmont continued, "where you might have observed activity in the pasture?"

"No, sir."

"Didn't you go to the stable to get the carriage which took you to London?" questioned Constable Jones.

"Yes, but that was a brief bit of business of no consequence," Quigg replied. "I saw nothing because I was looking for nothing."

"And you returned the carriage to the stable?" asked Piedmont.

"No. Alister Tweedly put it and the horses away," Quigg replied coolly, in complete control.

"The girl, Adriane Ornby, had been dead a good twelve hours before her body was found," Piedmont stated.

"That strikes me odd, sir," Quigg commented.

"Odd? In what way?"

"If I may observe, sir, there are animals in the pasture. The geese go sailing through periodically, and the cows grazing. While geese are not predators, I have seen them molest dead flesh. Had Miss Ornby's body been molested?"

"Her clothing was not in great disarray, although her gown was torn in a place or two," Piedmont informed, curious as to what Quigg was driving at. "She had flesh missing from her neck, just as Sara Cornhill had. Otherwise she did not appear as if she had been abused by animals."

"Then I would suggest that she had not been lying in the pasture all those twelve hours before she was discovered, that is all," Quigg said.

"I was just going to say the same thing," Constable Jones inserted as he stroked his belly.

"You believe she was carried or dragged to the pasture, perhaps only a short time before she was discovered?" Stopp questioned.

"I don't believe anything about the matter one way or

another, sir," Quigg replied. "I was simply offering an opinion."

"Very well." Piedmont Stopp cleared his throat. "If you have no further opinions, you may be excused, Quigg."

"I have none, and thank you, sir." Quigg went directly to the door, his back held straight as a board. He closed the door behind him.

"What do you think, Inspector Stopp?" asked Lord Henry.

Piedmont Stopp put a finger to his lips and crept on tiptoes to the door. He opened it stealthily to observe Quigg moving down the hallway, his posture and step not relaxed from the moment he left the room. Closing the door, Stopp turned into the room.

"I trust his story. Quigg is a good and efficient man," the inspector remarked. "Furthermore, he has a good head on him. I liked his deduction. I was observing his feet. They are remarkably small for such an imposing man. While he was here, I compared his feet with each of ours—and his were the smallest of the lot—but not abnormally small."

"Meaning?" Dr. Cummings asked, shaking himself from his attitude of daydreaming as he gazed into his glass of brandy.

"When these other gentlemen, with the aid of the stableman and groom, carried Miss Ornby's body back to the house," Piedmont explained, "I had a look about and discovered several exceptionally large footprints leading to the site and going beyond it in the direction of the woods, or perhaps the farms beyond. But the footsteps had come from the direction of the manor; and, upon careful examination, I noted they sunk deeper into the soft soil between the house and the place Adriane

Ornby was found, than they were leading off over the pasture. That brings me to believe that the individual possessor of those feet was carrying a substantial weight from the manor, but was free of it when he went beyond."

"From my examination," Dr. Cummings said, "I would have guessed that she had been carried, not dragged from where she had been strangled. It was all too clean to have happened in the pasture. As was, I might incidentally add, the body of Sara Cornhill."

"Most peculiar set of circumstances, I should say," Lord Henry commented.

"I found one further bit of evidence, perhaps," Stopp thought aloud. "The bloodied part of the front of a man's blouse. The material was coarsely woven the likes of which these country men wear. Since it was ripped from top to tail, I would surmise that it was a rather large shirt."

Lord Henry Weston snapped his fingers. "By Jove, that's it! The whole thing is as clear as spring water. The killing of Adriane was a revenge killing by the Cornhills. Both Ira and Jim are teased about their big feet—and they are large. That might explain why Adriane appeared to have been murdered in an identical way to Sara Cornhill."

"Lord Henry has a point there," Dr. Cummings interjected.

"Although I don't much like admitting it, I have to agree with his theory," Constable Jones said. "I would say our next move would be to go get Ira and Jim Cornhill and have a talk with them."

"Precisely what I was thinking, Constable," Stopp said. "Why don't you go fetch them and we'll interrogate them here?"

Constable Jones paled. He had always avoided conflict with either of the Cornhills, even when there was evidence pointing to the fact they might have not been on the up and up. "Perhaps we should all go and question them at their place. There's safety in numbers."

Dr. Cummings led the laughter. "You boys go on, I've got to get back to my practice."

Led by Constable Sedley Jones, R. Piedmont Stopp and Lord Henry Weston went about three kilometers beyond Merrihew Manor, and to the north, to where the Cornhill property was located. They were farmers with several tillable acres and livestock. Far from being affluent, they managed to get along. Chickens scattered as they arrived, making a raucous noise. Dogs barked and ran out to nip at the stranger's legs.

"Ira Cornhill!" Stopp yelled. "Call your dogs off. We want to speak with you."

The house was patched and in need of repair, as were the other buildings on the property. Ira Cornhill was a scraggly peasant with an unruly appearance. Thinly constructed, he hardly seemed the father of the strapping Jim Cornhill. He had dog eyes that were suspicious and at the same time sad. Mud-incrusted boots were observed by all three men as he came around the house screaming at the dogs.

"What brings ye?" Ira asked, wiping his hands on his trousers. "Ye're tresspassin', ye know, an' that goes for ye, too, Constable."

"We wish to speak to you and your son Jim," Jones managed to say.

"Speak to me all ye like," Ira rejoined, "but me Jim ain't 'ere."

"Not here?" questioned Stopp. "Where is he?"

"Gone, 'e ain't been 'ere since yesterday sometime. I

just cum 'ome a little bit ago," Ira informed. "Been up to Widow Gably's house butcherin' an 'og. The woman said that Jim ain't been 'ere since yesterday."

"Where does Widow Gably live?"

"Twelve kilometers further north o' 'ere, Constable. Ye know that. What was it ye wanted to talk to me about?"

"Widow Gably will vouch for your being there?"

"Ay, she will. I went up yesterday evenin' an' spent th' night with th' ol' crone as part o' th' bargain. She give me half a side o' pork an' a few coins to spare." He laughed jovially.

"The man is telling the truth," Stopp stated.

"O' course, I am!"

"Mr. Cornhill, when your son Jim comes home," Stopp instructed, "tell him to stop by Constable Jones' office. He'll have some questions to ask him."

"Questions? 'Bout what?"

"The death of your Sara, Mr. Cornhill. Come along."

"Jim never kilt his sister, if'n that's what ye're sayin'."

"That's not it, Mr. Cornhill; but you tell him to come along. And you might accompany him, if you like."

"What do you make of that?" inquired Lord Henry Weston as they arrived back at Merrihew Manor.

"Cornhill had too much proof of his whereabouts," Stopp said. "Besides he strikes me as a basically honest man."

"And what of Jim Cornhill?" asked Constable Jones.

"I think we had better all be on the lookout for Jim," Stopp declared. "He might be in hiding somewhere. Now you'd better round up some men, Constable, because we're liable to have a manhunt on our hands. In the meantime, Lord Henry, may I suggest that you ride in and see the vicar to make arrangements for funeral services tomorrow?"

"That would be the least I could do," Lord Henry commented. "You know, I can't get over the size of that man's feet." He whistled low.

"Funny, you should mention that, Lord Henry," Piedmont remarked, "because I've been having difficulty getting them from my mind, too."

CHAPTER FOURTEEN

Matthew Bienville arrived back at Merrihew Manor in the late afternoon, with his man Joply driving the carriage as usual. He went into the house from the rear entrance since he rode to the stable with Joply. The servant remained with Alister and Toby to acquire their assistance in cleaning the carriage and preparing it for an early departure.

Before entering the house, Matthew took time to survey the area with broad sweeping glances. His attention lingered for some time in the region of the pasture. Then he looked about the backside of the mansion, observing that three entrances were in view. Curiosity risen, he was tempted to go investigate as if the rear entrances were of significance to him. However, the door where he stood was thrown open and Mrs. Sharlock appeared in full stoic force. Glaring at him, Matthew flushed and felt guilty for no particular reason other

than that the woman possessed an insinuating stare.
They stood a moment as if they were squaring off, uncertain who was to speak first.

"Oh, it's you, Mr. Bienville," the woman said thickly,
her voice in a low, almost growling register. "Miss Phenwick said we were to expect you."

"Yes. I was detained on business a bit longer than I
thought I might be," Matthew replied. He tried a smile,
but got only a stone-cold reaction. "Things appear very
quiet here today."

"The mood has become more serene since the excitement of midday," she announced, gripping her hands
tightly at her waist.

"The excitement of midday? Ah, then Adriane has returned?"

"She has been found . . ."

"That is good news."

". . . *dead*," the housekeeper almost hissed.

"Dead?" Matthew stepped forward. Curiously, however, he glanced back at the pasture and the stable
as if he were expecting Joply.

"The vicar was here a short while ago making arrangements for tomorrow afternoon," the housekeeper informed. "I will prepare the body this evening. She will
lay in the chapel until tomorrow. The grave will be dug
tomorrow morning. Had I had my way, Ira Cornhill
would have been sent for to perform that task. He is
the best gravedigger, among other things, in these parts.
But there are sufficient workers about the place to hol-
low such a hole."

The moribund monologue was beginning to annoy
Matthew. Not that he was queasy especially, still he did
not like dwelling on such gruesome topics. He had
mounting concern about Joanne. "I'm certain that's all

very interesting, Mrs. Sharlock. However, I am fatigued from my travels. If you will excuse me."

Matthew went directly to the room which had been assigned to him. There he took time to sponge himself, douse scented water and change into fresh attire. Choosing an outfit in shades of blue to flatter his coloring, he appeared extremely dapper and desirable as he approached Joanne's rooms.

Joanne fell into his arms. She had been waiting so long, it seemed, for him to return from London. She wanted only to be held and lightly caressed. For some time they stood in that embrace by the large window overlooking the pasture and stable. As he stroked her, Matthew glanced again at the stable and the surrounding area. A few moments later Joply appeared at the door to the stable, accompanied by Toby and Alister. The stableman led the way to the pasture to show Matthew's man where the body of Adriane had been found.

"This must be very difficult for you, Joanna," commented Matthew a short while later, after they had positioned themselves comfortably before the blazing fire.

"I had a premonition when Lydia first told me that her sister was missing," Joanne returned, snuggling close to the man, "that Adriane would not be found alive. She just wasn't the type to go off by herself or even in the company of anyone that she did not know perfectly well. Lydia perhaps, not Adriane. But I'm not morbidly depressed. Despite the fact that I spent considerable time with my cousins, I was never particularly close to them—nor was I unnecessarily fond of either of them. Frankly, I pray that Lydia will quickly return to the United States."

"Good. I was afraid you might be tremendously upset by this," Matthew said, accompanied by a tiny kiss to her forehead. "In that case, I have a suggestion that we go into London this evening, have a sumptuous supper and take in a theatrical production."

"Oh, Matthew, could we?"

"I spoke with a friend of mind this noon, by the name of Isaac Colton-Smith, who is a theatre owner and producer-director of dramatic productions. He said he would save a box for us up until curtain time, should I be able to convince you to attend."

"You've convinced me already," Joanne said eagerly. "But the tragedy—"

"I need to get away from this house for a short while," she replied. "I'm about to be suffocated in all the tension around here."

"Then prepare yourself instantly and I'll advise Joply that we are going," Matthew stated as he rose.

Joanne had never been one to mourn over anything or anyone. Death, if it came, perhaps caught her by surprise; other than that, she accepted such happenings as inevitable. As to violence and murder, she refused to dwell on such lest she attract them to herself.

The notion of going to London and with such a handsome escort intrigued Joanne no end. Selecting a yellow satin dress which Susannah had given her, she decided against skirts that were too bellowy. Still she was fashionable and would attract attention with the dress if she did not with her very presence—which was more to the point. Susannah had also given her a large amount of costume jewelry, which was not inexpensive, but was not of tremendous value. The pieces, for the most part, were lovely paste. She had been warned about wearing costly diamonds in London without the proper security.

When Matthew called at her rooms nearly an hour later, Joanne was ready. By then she was in the process of wrapping a three-quarter length ermine cape about her shoulders. Matthew let a low whistle escape his lips.

"They'll think you're the ruddy Queen herself attending the theatre," said he, "except the Queen isn't a fraction as beautiful as you. You're not wearing real diamonds, are you?"

"No," she laughed, "only paste."

"Attractive paste, and, oh, how they glitter," he remarked as he stepped to her to run his hands about the top of the ermine cape and around back. Soon she was in his arms and for that moment she forgot all else in the world but this man.

Joply urged the horses at a rapid speed over the country roads, which tossed the occupants of the carriage from side to side. Still they were happy, young and filled with daring. As the carriage pulled into the city, the driver found it prudent to set the horses at a slower pace.

Joanne sat close to Matthew. She was like a child anticipating a make-believe world. Lamps glistened, lights in shop windows, lanterns hand-carried. More and more lamps.

"Oh, Matthew, I've never seen such brilliance at night," she exclaimed. "I can hardly believe my eyes!"

"Enjoy it, precious Joanne. Enjoy and believe!"

"What will we do first?"

"Find a hotel. I have reservations at the Prince Edward."

"Reservations?" She cocked an eyebrow. "Why a hotel?"

"My dear Joanna, if we go to the theatre and have supper afterward," he said, "we won't be finished until the wee hours of the morning. That would be far too late to drive back to Merrihew, now wouldn't it? Didn't I mention that I had arranged for rooms?"

"No. If you had, I wouldn't have come along."

"Not even if they were two private rooms, one for you and one for me?"

Joanne laughed to cover nervousness. "That would make a vast difference."

"Now if you were a different sort of a girl," Matthew speculated, "a Sara Cornhill, for instance, you might bloody well jump at the opportunity to share a single room for an evening."

"Sara Cornhill? How do you know Sara Cornhill?" she asked suspiciously.

"Did I say Sara Cornhill?" He chuckled in an attempt at covering the error. "I meant to say Sally Thornhill—an actress of limited talent for the stage, but adequate to attract interest in her person."

Joanne looked directly at him. Flickering shadows made strange changing designs over his features. "Why *did* you say Sara Cornhill? I find that most peculiar."

Again an attempt at laughter. "I've heard a thing or two about Sara Cornhill from the local boys about Merrihew Manor. She was no convent nun."

Joanne did not persist with questions, but she still was suspicious of his reference to the name.

The carriage pulled up before the Prince Edward Hotel. Lamps were brightly blazing at the entranceway. A man in a red doorman's outfit came to the door of the carriage and assisted Joanne to the carpet which ran to the curb. He gave Matthew a hand as well. Passers-by stopped abruptly to admire the handsome couple, who were instantly mistaken for royalty. They grandly left the street and entered the posh lobby. Crystal. Reflected light. Mirrors. Potted plants. Richly ornate furniture.

Thick carpeting. Elegant people posturing in fashionable attire as if they were on display. Diamonds, real and paste, that were indistinguishable one from the other. Artistic-looking people. Aristocrats. Pretenders. Largely older individuals. An occasional young thing on the arm of an affluent-appearing man. To Joanne they were all Lords and Ladies, Kings and Queens as she knew such to be from her childhood days of fantasy.

The rooms were acquired and the bellman took them to the lift to be transported to the third floor. The rooms were not together, an arrangement that they would have to accept because of the lateness of the reservation.

Joanne's room was small but sufficient. Now she liked the idea of spending the night in London. Matthew had gone to his room to arrange his things with Joply.

She spun about the room, twirling her skirt as she did. The bellman had lit two lamps. Turning one out, she stood in semi-darkness and posed before a large mirror, checking the dangle of her jewelry in the process.

The room was stuffy. Going to the window, she pushed the draperies back. An alley was below with another three-story building immediately next to it. She had recalled passing a hotel just before the carriage pulled up to the Prince Edward, and it was not as nice. Lighted windows. Some with the draperies pulled back. Breathing deeply of the fresh night air, she felt even more exhilarated and already had forgotten Matthew's reference to Sara Cornhill. Yet she had second thoughts about the man and particularly about being in London alone with him. After all, what did she know about him? He was a handsome stranger who came to Merrihew Manor during a storm and asked for a place to stay the night. He told her many things about himself; but couldn't they have been contrived and narrated in such a way that would be beneficial to his purpose.

His purpose? Indeed, what was his purpose? Certainly he was a worldly man who had traveled extensively and had a charming way with people. Could he not simply be an opportunist, a handsome person who gained the confidence of other persons for some ulterior motive? Why did such questions persist?

She liked the man. Perhaps she could like him very much. Yet because he had mentioned the name of Sara Cornhill—supposedly by mistake—she had become suspicious, questioning, anxious. Indeed she did like him and looked forward to being with him. Why the fear? Why the uncertainty? She must learn more about him before they returned to Merrihew Manor.

Standing silhouetted by the window, she cast a glance at the bed large enough for two. He had been romantic and exciting, but always the proper gentleman with her at Merrihew, politely knowing the precise moment to ease his caressing, his delicious kisses, to move away to disconnect the physical contact that could only build to one ultimate conclusion. She had never progressed to that degree with any man. Could that possibly be his purpose for bringing her to London, his motivation, ulterior desire? This was not the first time that thought had flickered through her mind, but this time she gave it serious consideration. She would simply have to be on her guard, let him know early that that was not her desire.

A light was lit in the room directly across the alley from hers. Instantly she could tell that it was nowhere near as nice as the hotel in which she was staying. In fact, *shabby* would fairly well describe it. A lumbering shadow could be seen. Curiously she watched as a man emerged from the shadows, pulling a blouse over his head. The candle glowed over his bare skin. Then when the blouse was thrown aside, she could see the man's face. It was Jim Cornhill! Quickly she turned away and pulled the draperies closed.

Had he seen her? Of that she could not be certain. Even if he had, would he recognize her in the costume she was wearing? Perhaps. Still she believed that she had been hidden in shadows, only visible a fleeting moment.

She was relieved to hear Matthew's knock at the door and, mustering a light attitude, gaily ran to answer it.

CHAPTER FIFTEEN

Matthew had rushed her with, "It's almost curtain time. Being fashionably late is one thing, having to grope for one's seat is another." She put the sight of Jim Cornhill momentarily from her mind. The rush, the glitter, the excitement were for that time more important than anything else to her.

Grandly they sat in the theatre box, in view of the audience only seconds before the curtain was to rise. Eyes observed them. Whispers. Opinions. Candid exclamations. Matthew sat proudly, observing the reaction from the corner of his vision, pleased to be seen with such a ravishing creature. Joanne was beside herself with enthusiasm. Sparkling eyes, joyous smile, feeling a little silly and uninhibited. She could be no more delighted unless she herself were to be one of the performers upon the stage.

Joanne was quickly absorbed in the melodramatic

story being performed before her. She identified with
the heroine, played by an older actress pretending to be
a sweet young thing. The older suitor was a man of
minor nobility with a lecherous attitude toward the heroine; in fact, his lechery was directed at all young
females from mid-childhood upward. The hero was magnificently handsome and conceited with a marvelous profile, a nose copied from an ancient Roman coin. He
postured and gesticulated as a hero should, dashingly
sweeping the heroine off her feet. Then there was minor
conflict between the character actresses and more intrigue. The excitement climaxed in the final act when
the character actress with the aquiline nose revealed
the truth about the villainous noble and his perverted
ways. Her testimony saved the hero, who then rushed to
the arms of the waiting heroine. Before the great revela-
tion, Joanne had become so moved by the plight of the
hero and heroine that she was overpowered by emotions
and wept. Then, so relieved that the two were once
again happily united, she applauded merrily and had to
exercise control to keep from shouting out her enthusiasm.

During the two intermissions, Matthew had created
quite a sensation by introducing Joanne around to the
more influential patrons of the theatre. He declined
several offers of parties, explaining that they were having an intimate supper in a very private dining room.
Eyes raised. Men chuckled with distant memories.
Ladies tried to be tolerant and understanding. Joanne
naively did not comprehend the insinuation, or at least
she was oblivious to it. Creating such a sparkling display,
she was the center of attention without trying.

"Joanna, permit me to introduce Mr. Isaac Colton-
Smith," Matthew said when he could catch her atten-

tion in the theatre lobby. "Mr. Colton-Smith is not only the owner of this theatre, but he is also the producer and artistic director of the play."

Joanne's eyes twinkled as she smilingly turned to greet the man. Her smile did not diminish, nor her interest, when she discovered the portly man of about fifty years standing beside Matthew. Clad in evening clothes, his cravat appeared a bit too tight and caused him to have an extra-large double chin below his round expressive face. Black cape, long flowing brown and silver hair, an artistically large nose, curiously sensual lips, eyes that were afire with intensity. Sucking in his breath, his chest expanded and his trousers sagged. With courtly manners he reached for her hand and bowed low.

"Miss Phenwick, I am perfectly charmed," he said in grandly executed tones, enunciating each syllable as if it were precious.

"Why, thank you, Mr. Smith," she returned with only a hint of a curtsy. "It is my honor."

"The name is Colton-Smith," he pronounced. "I'm hyphenated, you know."

"I'm terribly sorry, Mr. Colton-Smith." This time she curtsied.

"A natural mistake, dear lady. One doesn't wear one's hyphen on one's sleeve, you know," the portly man explained. "Besides, between the two of us, it is pretty much an affectation. But don't tell a soul I mentioned it." He cleared his throat pompously. "Mr. Bienville tells me you are interested in acting."

"I'm overwhelmed. Why, the heroine actually moved me to tears," she confessed.

"No, that is not precisely what I meant," Colton-Smith corrected. "Bienville informs me that you have an interest in acting yourself, performing, as it were."

"Oh, indeed, yes. After tonight I am more than convinced of that," she uttered.

"I suppose you've heard that it is a wicked life," the man commented to gain her reaction.

"Any life can be wicked if one makes it so," she returned sweetly.

"Here, here," he exclaimed. "Yes, I think you have much to offer the theatre. We must discuss the subject at length."

Matthew interrupted as the large man appeared to be moving too close to the girl. "At another time, Isaac. Miss Phenwick and I have extensive plans for the remainder of the evening."

"Oh, I see. Perhaps she would like to meet the members of the company," Colton-Smith suggested with a twinkle.

"At another time," stated Matthew firmly. "You will excuse us now, we have reservations for supper."

"But I should have enjoyed meeting the company of actors, Matthew," she remarked as they stepped into the carriage. "They all seemed like such interesting individuals."

"Interesting, yes. And individuals, yes. Still negative things can be interesting; not that I mean to imply these people are not worth knowing. Certainly, if you are serious about wanting to be an actress, you will have to associate with such people," Matthew told her.

They rode only a short distance before they reached the very exclusive restaurant and were led to the private dining room. The small chamber was elegantly decorated. Light oak paneling, intricately carved. A large beveled mirror. Flowers. Upholstered furniture and an intimate table set for two.

Matthew took her cape, lightly kissing her at the back

of the neck as he did. She reacted as the heroine on the stage had responded to the hero's kiss. Already she was playacting. She practically spun into the room, grandly surveying it.

"I've never seen a room quite like this," she articulated, conscious of her speech. "I didn't even know such places existed."

"This is the sort of place a wealthy earl or duke or prince might bring a lady of his fascination," Matthew informed, playacting too, "for a clandestine occasion of sensual pleasure."

"Is that why you've brought me here?"

"It is a thought."

"Yet one you had best dismiss," Joanne returned, insistence in her voice.

An exchange of glares and Matthew knew she meant what she said. "I was only jesting."

"I trust that is the truth, Matthew," she said. "I like you very much, and find you extremely interesting. Still I have certain moral values. I suppose that sounds contradictory when I say I want to be an actress, since such creatures have sordid reputations to begin with. But I am different."

"I'll admit I've known one or two with—" He cleared his throat. "—interesting reputations that made them quite delightful. Yet I will not pursue the matter further." He indicated the room. "Shall we dine first?"

"First? Before what?"

"Before we relax—and have a *platonic* conversation." He laughed, but there was cynicism in his voice.

"I'm quite famished."

Matthew ordered for the two of them, sparing no expense in an attempt at impressing her. Then after the wine arrived, he proposed a toast to her career as an actress.

"Now then, what shall we talk about?" he asked, trying to ascertain where her thoughts were.

"A curious question comes to mind, which I've been meaning to ask you about," Joanne said, staring him directly in the eyes.

"And that is—"

"Why, on the first night you spent at Merrihew Manor, you and your man Joply were seen in the pasture in the wee hours of the morning?" she asked as a matter of fact.

Matthew was caught slightly off guard. "Whoever told you such a thing?"

"The stableman. He saw you."

"Oh, that, Joanna." He laughed uneasily. "Something had awakened Joply. He is a light sleeper and is plagued with terrifying dreams. He came to my room and told me about his discomforture, explaining he had awakened from a nightmare and glanced out the window and saw something or someone roaming about in the pasture. Since he thought it had some connection with the dream that had just terrified him, he would not be pacified until I went out with him to have a look. Assuring him that it was all his imagination, after we had made the messy trip to the pasture, he finally went back to his room and slept the rest of the night. That is all it was. I was surprised that such a move was noticed."

Joanne felt that he was not telling the truth, that he had contrived a rather absurd story. Still she would not challenge him further at that time and perhaps ruin a lovely evening.

"I told Alister it was of no consequence," Joanne lied,

"and that there was a simple, logical explanation for it."

"There, you see, you were correct, Joanna. I'm impressed." Matthew poured more wine. "You're lovely when there's a question in your eyes."

"My life has been filled with asking questions," she replied, "with few exceptions from Great-uncle Uriah, a wonderful old doctor, and Rosea Hackleby, a person you have to meet to appreciate, to the most common domestic servant. Isn't that what life is all about: asking questions?"

Matthew smiled broadly. "I think some time, perhaps a considerable amount of it, should be spent in answering them. The questions are only half of the game."

Joanne laughed. "Shall we play questions and answers?"

"I love it when you laugh, Joanna."

"That was a statement, neither a question nor an answer." She laughed even more, beginning to perceive the effects of the wine.

"Right. So life is also concerned with making statements," Matthew returned. "But that statement might have been in answer to an unspoken question; or perhaps it was expressed to provoke a question."

Dinner lasted two hours, each course luxuriously served and lingered over while the two people got to know each other. Matthew was content to play the game according to her rules for the time being, certain that his masculine charm would win her over in time to come. Still he was basically a patient man who had often waited for some desired treasure to discover that his perseverance proved fruitful. He enjoyed the pursuit, the cat-and-mouse ploy.

After dinner, lightheaded with rich food and potent

wine, Joanne was less inhibited, freer with her words and her physical expressions. Still she remained in control of her faculties while giddily enjoying the situation. Matthew, too, had become more cheerful, laughing loudly at trivia and feeling completely at ease.

Kisses were exchanged. But when it appeared that a seriousness descended upon them, it was Joanne who had to purposefully maintain control and divert his enthusiasm.

At nearly two A.M. the handsome couple left the private dining room and asked that their carriage be sent for. Still lighthearted and giddy and finding everything humorous, they waited in the elegantly decorated foyer.

"Ah, my gloves!" exclaimed Matthew, as if he had forgotten his greatest treasure. "I left them in the dining room."

"Can't you send someone?" asked Joanne.

"It'll only take a moment. You wait here for Joply and the carriage." Before Joanne could object, he had taken flight and immediately disappeared from sight.

A few moments later, as Joanne stood in the cool morning air to refresh and revive herself, the carriage arrived. Joply assisted her into the vehicle.

"Thank you, Joply," she said as she fell back against the seat. "Mr. Bienville will be here momentarily."

Joply smiled understandingly. Yet his eyes were searching about her to the extent that it began to make her nervous.

Lightly she asked, "Had any good dreams lately?"

"How's that?"

"Have you had any good dreams?" She giggled.

"No, Miss. I don't dream."

"Never?"

"If I do, I don't recall. They've quite vanished when I awaken."

"Not even nightmares?"

"Never nightmares. I'm certain I would recall those since I've heard others relate about such things. Why do you ask?"

Joanne shook her head. "No reason." She glanced up to see Matthew coming through the door. "That will be all, Joply."

Joply stared curiously at her for a moment before stepping back to permit Matthew to enter.

"Shall we ride around for awhile? See London at this time of night?" inquired Matthew lightly.

"No. I think I need to get some rest . . . some sleep. I've become quite exhausted," she replied.

"We could ride about with your head upon my shoulder, my arm about you."

"I prefer that you simply take me back to the hotel and deposit me at my room," she insisted. "It's far too late for taking a ride. I'm only fresh from the country, unused to city ways."

"Whatever you say, my dear," Matthew returned, trying to conceal disappointment. He gave Joply instructions to take them directly to the hotel.

At her door, Matthew made one valiant attempt to obtain entrance for a final romantic interlude. By then, however, she was in full control of her senses and only too well aware that she had caught Matthew in an obvious falsification. She permitted a good night kiss, but it was brief and without passionate overtones.

Moments later she was in her room, the door closed and locked. Still the fascinating picture of the man lingered—along with the thought that he had not told the truth about being in the pasture at Merrihew that night.

Still she was just curious enough to wait it out and discover what he was up to.

Later, as she prepared for bed, she received the distinct impression that either she was not alone in the room, or that someone had been in it prior to her returning. Why did she have that feeling?

She extinguished the lamp and went to the window. Pulling back the draperies, she gazed across the alley to the room where she had seen Jim Cornhill. A covering was over the window and the room appeared dark.

Asleep?

CHAPTER SIXTEEN

The hotel room was gyrating around her, giving the impression that it had suddenly become spherical. Lying flat on the bed only made the hallucination worse. Cool water to her forehead and a soothing cloth once she had removed her dress. Wearing only her undergarments, which were elegant enough to pass for outerwear, she wrapped her cape about her in a mixed reaction to spasms of chill, then flushes of heat. Giggling for no reason, she flopped gracelessly into a large comfortable chair. Not quite as she would like it, she dragged another chair to the first to use to rest her feet upon. In that position she drifted off into brief sleep.

As rapidly as she lost consciousness, she regained it about thirty minutes later. Now a slight pounding in her head, blurry vision and a let-down sensation. Managing to get water, she drank a goodly amount without resting for air. She wandered back to the chair and fell into it again. Awake, she tried sorting her thoughts, remembering events of the evening. There was actually a period of time after supper in that private dining room during which she could not recall fully what had happened. That blank bothered her. As she puzzled, thoughts returned to the theatrical performance she had attended. That event was still very vivid in her mind.

In the alcoholically drugged recesses of her mind, the situations and characters of the play presented themselves in abnormally perverted images. And as she considered the plot, she saw a resemblance between the villain and Lord Henry Weston. Although the actor played it with a broad style of gesturing, pronouncing the words and projecting his licentious self to the audience, still she found a remarkable similarity; yet she did not know why that was the case since Lord Henry had never presented himself in that light to her. If anything he was somewhat reserved. Still she could not dismiss the feeling.

The more she dwelled on the matter, the more perplexed she became. She had to discuss it with someone. Could it wait until morning? Perhaps. However, she was now wide awake as if that brief nap would suffice her for the next several hours.

She paced about the room. It had stopped its spiraling movement. Another drink of cool water. Twice she glanced out the window across the way to see if there was any activity in the room in which she had seen Jim Cornhill. She beheld only blackness.

Checking her appearance in a mirror, she was convinced that no one but her dressmaker would suspect her undergarment was not just a simple item of outer wearing apparel. Besides, with the cape over it, who could possibly suspect?

Her intention was to go immediately to Matthew's room, wake him and discuss her theories about the play. As she reached the corridor outside, she realized she did not know the exact number or whereabouts of his room. Descending the stairs, she went to the main desk to secure that information. The clerk, who wore tiny glasses and had a very shiny head, glanced over the spectacles with a look that could be nothing but suspicious and then insinuating. Prissily he discharged the room number and motioned for a boy to assist her to the lift. However, that apparatus was not in working operation, so she ended by reclimbing the stairs, stopping several times en route as the pounding in her head became more severe.

Joanne examined the piece of paper with Matthew's room number scrawled upon it. Fearing that she might awaken other hotel guests, she rapped as quietly as she could. No response. Again. Still no response.

The awkward-looking bellboy, who would have taken her in the lift, had been sent to follow her by the suspicious night clerk. His large loop of keys made a noisy jangling sound as he approached her.

"You'll disturb the other guests," he commented.

"But I can't seem to arouse Mr. Bienville," she reported, then contrived, "I'm concerned about him. He wasn't feeling well when we returned to the hotel."

The boy with the plain countenance looked almost blankly at her. "Mr. Bienville and his valet left at least half an hour ago, or longer."

"That's impossible!" she stated a bit irrationally. "I know he's in his room."

Not one to indulge in extensive arguments, the boy found the proper key on the loop, pushed it into the keyhole and turned. An instant later the door swung into the room. Judiciously the boy lit a lamp from a small box of matches he carried with him. Quite so, the room was not occupied, the bed had not been disturbed. Still, with a glance about, it was easy to determine that he had left most of his things there.

"If you care to look," the boy said coldly, "you may examine the quarters assigned to the valet. However, I know for a fact that they both left together."

"No. Thank you. I will accept your word," Joanne replied. Again the dizziness and throbbing in her head.

The boy left. Joanne returned to her room. Puzzling while standing without the room, she turned back to see if the boy was still lurking in the shadows. The sight she saw was enough to startle her.

A ghostlike creature with wildly disarrayed hair came somnambulistically down the corridor, clad in a long, somewhat diaphanous gown of decidedly flimsy quality. The closer she came, the more demented she appeared, as if she were removed to another world. Muttering, making gestures that were far too large and sweeping for a woman of her years, she came nearer. Joanne put her back to the door and watched as terror filled her. Large protruding eyes blankly scanned, darting in first one direction, then another. Twisted fingers, long and expressive, formed artistic patterns as they swept through the air. Bracelets dangled with a dull clanking sound, and rings glistened at her fingers—obviously not real jewels. Her nose was prominent but magnificently carved with an aristocratic flair that made her appear to be some grand duchess or a queen mother. The long, supple face continuously altered as if every two or three words she muttered required a change of facial expression.

As the older woman was within little more than arm's

length of Joanne, she recognized her as the character actress who had appeared in the theatrical production she
had seen that evening. The great pale blue eyes rolled
in the girl's direction and focused. The twisted fingers
froze in midair and her lips held on a single syllable.

The woman stared until Joanne became extremely un-
comfortable. She fumbled behind her for the doorknob,
but did not come close. The flickering light played grotesque shadows over each of their faces. It was the
woman who was first to gain her composure.

"I had no idea anyone in the entire world was up this
time of the morning," the woman pronounced grandly
with rich round tones that had a way of rumbling
through the girl. "My room is on the next floor. I'm a
permanent guest of the Prince Edward. However, for a
change of scene, I quite often walk through the other
floors this time of day. I'm ever so quiet and never disturb a soul."

"You're an actress, aren't you?" Joanne managed to
utter.

The woman's hand swung dramatically into the air as
if she were making a declaration. "I am. You have seen
me perform?"

"Yes, this evening."

"Ah, not one of my greatest roles," the woman with the
glorious vocal tones remarked, "but it is not one of the
worst, either. In younger days, when I was a leading lady,
I was really quite something else. Ah, the toast of London! Nay, the toast of the continent! Of Paris! Vienna!
All the great theatres adored me. You'll forgive my im-
modest attitude, but when one has been lavished with
the praise and adulation I have received, the tendency
to remember is difficult to suppress. I am Mrs. Lillian
Harper-Sharpe."

"Mrs. Lillian Harper-Sharpe! Of course, I remember your name from the programme. I loved your performance," Joanne said enthusiastically.

"You did? Oh, I am pleased," Mrs. Harper-Sharpe exclaimed. "Compliments are an actor's most cherished reward. Applause is the fuel that kindles the inner fire and gives a momentary satisfaction, but the spoken compliment is a form of ambrosia to the serious actor: it says that their job has been well done in a personal way. Mayn't I know your name, my dear?"

"Joanna Phenwick."

"Joanna? What a lovely name?"

While they were conversing, the bellboy came dashing up the stairs and hurried to them. "You are making far too much noise in the public hallway, ladies. Complaints are certain to be registered. You know, Mrs. Harper-Sharpe, the agreement you made with the desk clerk. You may trespass the halls with your nocturnal wanderings, but you are not to engage in conversation."

"This young lady, Miss Phenwick, was about to join me in my room for a glass of sherry," Mrs. Harper-Sharpe said grandly. "Weren't you, my dear?"

Joanne glanced at the grim expression on the youth's face and nodded her head in agreement. "We were just going, as a matter of fact."

Taking Mrs. Harper-Sharpe's arm, the two promenaded to the staircase leading up. The youth watched as they moved out of sight. Scratching his head, he shrugged and returned to his station.

The room was cluttered with mementoes from old theatre programmes to pictures, most of which had been executed with mediocre talent, to peacock feathers, books and theatre posters. Cheap jewelry was strewn everywhere as if it were considered part of the decora-

tion. The scent of ancient perfume hovered, mixed with
other odors, probably incense and moldy bread. Shawl
upon shawl was strewn across the furniture as if there
were no other place to put them, and they would add to
the color of the room anyway. The bed was old with
large mattresses and huge bolsters, giving the impression that one would instantly sink into the depth of
feathers and thus remain until hoisted out. The top-floor
room was not used by the choicest guests; it struck Joanne as being little more than a garret. Still it was home
to the elegant lady who occupied it.

The sherry was dispensed in ornate glasses which were
one of the treasures of the actress. Lillian sat leisurely
on a chaise, while Joanne occupied a patched chair
which was obviously an imitation of a Louis XIV design.
Still not completely at ease with the woman, Joanne
sipped the sherry and hoped it would do something for
the dizziness and general upset feeling she had earlier experienced.

"I suppose I abducted you, didn't I, Joanna? I didn't
mean to do anything so physical," Lillian commented,
"but that bellboy can be terribly annoying at times.
Were it my place, I would dismiss him on the spot! Alas,
it is not."

"He was a bit overbearing, wasn't he?" Joanne said.

"The management has changed over the years since
I've been a resident here," Lillian informed. "I think they
resent that I am a permanent guest of their hòstelry."

"A permanent guest?"

"Mr. Horatio Sharpe, who was my benefactor before
his demise, long ago made arrangements with this establishment, paying them an outrageous price, for me to
have lodgings here—these specific rooms—for the rest of
my life." Her great eyes rolled about and an expression

of brief sorrow elongated her face. "Alas, dear man, he has long since been in his grave. Yet what a wonderful liaison we had in those old and glorious days! I was still leading lady then, and he was frantically infatuated with me. I cannot call it love because I'm not certain what that mysterious word means. Still he was romantically everything a woman could have desired, both in public and in private."

"You married him?"

"No. I took his name and added it to my own, along with the title of Mrs. to make the matter appear legitimate," Lillian explained. "You see, there was another Mrs. Horatio Sharpe."

"Oh, I'm so sorry for you."

"Don't be sorry for me," Lillian responded. "I was the fortunate one. I only knew the beautiful side of Horatio Sharpe; I never had to put up with his illnesses and discomfortures, nor any of the other negative aspects of the man. And he well provided for me along with putting considerable monies into theatrical productions for me as principal actress. A lovely man! But let us not speak of the past. It is today, tonight or this morning, and the present is really the only tangible thing we have."

"I agree." Joanne was beginning to feel more at ease. "Have you been an actress all your life?"

"Most of it. I have been entertaining for as long as I can remember." Lillian became quiet for a moment as she studied the girl's face. "I perceive you have a curious interest in the theatre, my dear. Am I mistaken?"

"Not mistaken. I aspire to be an actress."

"How very interesting," Lillian remarked. "Yet you appear to come from some affluence."

"I do."

"I've never known any wealthy actresses," Lillian remarked, bouncing the tips of her fingers together. "Many a girl has thought to attract wealth through her beauty and dramatic ability; but none have been extremely successful. Oh, there was my Horatio Sharpe—who had a wife—but he was most generous. There were other admirers in my day. An actress often motivates a challenge in men that arouses them to action, as if they were attempting to prove their masculinity by devious means. Some men become addicted to actresses until other women hardly stimulate or amuse them. We are a breed unto ourselves. I don't know that you have that driving something it takes to make a successful actress. Actually, most of us have come from common surroundings and have simply imagined ourselves into exotic roles. We perfect our speech, learn the gestures, develop the technique of expressing emotions, assume the posture and suddenly we're grand ladies of the theatre. But you're a grand lady to begin with. Why would you want to step down to our existence?"

"I don't feel I would be stepping down," Joanne replied. "My cousin is Susannah Phenwick, the renowned concert pianist. Perhaps you've heard of her. She is a performer, an entertainer in her own way. I was never musically inclined, but I have been filled with the entertainer's spirit for as long as I can remember. I have three brothers, no sisters, and I was forever forcing them to play make-believe acting games with me. Gus and Prentise were not very good at it, but Joshua, the youngest, possesses an imagination to match my own. Oh, how we would dress up and act out stories we had read. Joshua is now in England, too, going to Elton School. He hasn't the aspirations I have."

"You come from a wealthy family? American?"

"Yes—to both questions. But I shan't let either stand in my way," she said with determination. Since she did not want to get into that topic with the woman who was hardly more than a stranger, she changed the trend of conversation. "Do you happen to know a man by the name of Matthew Bienville?"

"Matt Bienville?" Lillian chuckled. "Oh, yes, he is one who has appeared and disappeared around the theatre for years. A strikingly handsome man, he usually shows interest only in young actresses."

"Has he a notorious reputation?"

"With young ladies, yes. It seems he does not have great amounts of money, although he earns large sums from time to time," informed Lillian. "He puts in an appearance when he is in an affluent state. He invests heavily into our productions, and I suppose Mr. Colton-Smith is greatly indebted to him. If memory serves me, Lord Weston was the one who introduced him to our little group of players."

"Lord Henry Weston of Falcon Heath Castle?"

"The same. A dear, lecherous old man! You'll excuse that remark, but the man is quite a rounder." Lillian chuckled as past images danced into her mind. "Poor Lady Genevieve is suspicionless—or at least so one is led to believe. I think she is wiser than she pretends to be. We have become friendly, Lady Genevieve and I, since Lord Henry often invites the company to Falcon Heath for holiday in nice weather."

Joanne's lower lip dropped. "Do you mean to say that Lord Henry Weston and Matthew Bienville are friends?"

"I would augment that with the statement that they appear to be exceptionally good friends," Lillian stated.

"But they were both at Merrihew Manor the night before last," Joanne explained, "and neither seemed to know the other as I recall. Perhaps that was only an impression they gave." Her thoughts were no longer with Mrs. Lillian Harper-Sharpe; instead they had returned to that night. A stab of apprehension shot through her.

CHAPTER SEVENTEEN

Joanne's mind was racing with confusion. Finding difficulty concentrating on her conversation with Mrs. Lillian Harper-Sharpe, she asked to be excused with promise of continuing at another time. The actress pronounced a long goodbye with hopes that they would become friends in the near future and suggestions that they have luncheon together the next time Joanne was in London.

Hurriedly she returned to her room on the third floor, taking the steps rapidly. She remembered that she had not locked her door and that caused her further anxiety. Reaching the room, she found that indeed the door was unlocked. She pushed into the room and fastened the door behind her. The one candle which she had left burning was out. Not surprising since it was small when she lit it earlier. Where were the matches? She searched about in the usual place, but did not find them.

Lunging toward the draperies, she pulled them back

and hoped for moonlight. Very little. Still some ligh
came into the room. She hesitated as she noticed th
window across the alley was uncovered and a tiny flick
er of light was visible within. Curiously she stood o
tiptoes in hopes of seeing more of the room. The be
was obscured from her view. Deciding that it was bes
she get some sleep, she could undress in the dark an
not worry about candlelight the rest of the night. Afte
casting the cape aside, her eyes adjusting to the dark
ness, she returned to the window and craned again t
see into the opposite room.

"Lookin' for someone, were ye, lass?" came a voic
out of the blackness.

Joanne jumped, squealed and nearly fainted on th
spot. "Who—who is it?"

"Who ye be lookin' for across the way, ain't there," h
stated and she was certain she recognized the voice.

"Jim Cornhill?"

"Ay, ye know me voice."

"What are you doing in my room?"

"I've come for a bit o' a visit, if'n ye don't mind."

Now she could see the outline of features on his inter
esting, if not altogether handsome face. "But I do mind
You're trespassing at a disrespectful hour."

"What is so disrespectful about this hour, lass?" Jin
asked, reaching a hand to touch her shoulder.

She jerked away from his touch and plunged towar
the door. Yanking at the knob, she discovered the doo
was locked and the key was not in the keyhole wher
she had left it. "What have you done with my key?"

" 'Tis in safe keepin', lass. I saw ye viewin' across th
alley into me room several times. I thought I shoul
present meself to ye in person if'n ye were so anxious to
behold me manly self."

She backed away from him. "I thought I recognized you. I simply wished to ascertain that it was you, Jim Cornhill. What are you doing in London?"

"Perhaps I come a-lookin' for ye, lass."

"Then you'd better go back home. I don't want to look at you." Fear was now charging through her with terrifying force.

Jim struck a match and lit a candle. The eerie glow gave him a sinister expression. "I think nay 'till later, lass. 'Tis a fine place ye have here, nay like that pigsty o' a room across th' bloomin' way. If'n I have th' key, an' there be no other way o' gettin' from this room, I do nay know why ye are runnin' about all in a frenzy. Ye're like a chicken in a house when a fox comes to call. Ye'll get your feathers all rumpled."

"Matthew Bienville is in the next room," she lied. "I have but to knock on the wall and he'll be in here in an instant."

"The gentleman ye mentioned may have rented the room next door," Jim said confidently, "but he ain't in there."

"And I have an older lady friend in the room directly above," she contrived, "who hears the slightest sounds of protest from me and she will have the management here before you can unlock that door."

Jim chuckled loudly. "Ye checked into this hotel with a man, lass. Perhaps ye took separate rooms, but there is nay reason ye must use the two. Ay, I'll be man enough for ye—seein' as how your other man went off awhile back with his man in th' carriage. Now then, where d'ye suppose they be off to, lass, at this time o' th' night?"

"I—I don't know."

"Ye're quite alone, lass. An' ye need me."

"I need *you?* Whatever for?"

"Because I be a familiar face, I do, an' a lad, despite his bloody physical desire for ye, who cares a mite for your future."

"You contradict yourself," she said, trying another tactic.

"I nay understand your meanin'."

"If you have any concern for my future," she stated, "you would not consider the base desires which must be rattling around in your head at this moment. I could never respect a man who sought to take his pleasure from me against my wishes."

"Then perchance with a wee bit o' sweet talk an' friendly persuasion, ye might change your wishes, lass." He stepped closer.

She backed against the bedpost and took a desperate measure. "Did you kill my cousin Adriane?"

The question caught him off guard. "Did I *what*?"

"Did you kill my cousin Adriane? She was found in the identical spot your sister was found in the pasture," Joanne stated.

Jim fell back, reaching for a chair to brace himself. "Your cousin is dead?"

"Yes. Her body was found this afternoon," Joanne informed. "There is suspicion that *you* killed her."

"Me?"

"As revenge for your own sister's death."

Jim wanted to laugh contemptuously, but his throat was filled with conflicting emotion. A meaty hand wiped across his face, brushing back his hair in a continuous movement. "Would ye believe me if'n I told ye I didn't?"

"Why should I when you demonstrate you are the kind of ruthless man you have shown me here tonight?" she fired.

"Ruthless?"

"Coming in here with the intention of taking whatever you want from me. Only an animal behaves that way."

"Then every man I know is an animal," he sighed, shaking his head.

"I have no respect for a man who does not behave as a gentleman," she returned, an edge of anger in her voice. "You are a good-looking man, Jim Cornhill; but no self-respecting girl would have a thing to do with a man like your behavior indicates you must be."

"No lass has ever talked to me like what ye are," he confessed, a tone of contriteness coming to his voice. "D'ye try to make me out a fool, lass?"

"I can never make you out to be anything you aren't to begin with," she threw back. "If you want me to take you for being a fool, then express yourself as one. If you touch a hair of my head, foolishly attempt to get your way with me, then you had best kill me, for if I live beyond such an encounter, I will see that you are prosecuted and receive the maximum punishment—which, I should imagine, would be death by hanging. Think on that, Jim Cornhill, then attack me if you will."

Jim stared, his eyes growing large, then squinting to mere slits. Lips puckered to express words, but sound would not come. His expression was one of disbelief. The candlelight flickered in the fine layer of perspiration that came to his brow. Now gruntlike sounds, faint moans, quickening of breath. Finally a burst of merry laughter. "Ay, ye do be a spunky one, don't ye? I've never had a go-round with th' likes o' ye before. Ye make th' quest far more worth th' effort, if'n I do say so."

"The quest?"

One eye opened slightly and he appeared to be studying her with it alone, as if gaining perspective. "Ay, lass, the quest—an' th' conquest. Ye're quite a lady, I have to give ye that. Ye're th' prettiest lady I've ever set me eyes upon, an' I hope never to see another prettier." He sighed. "Give me th' common lass with the none too pretty features, the curious simple ways, who have no ambitions but what to bring out th' animal in men—as ye was sayin'. Ay, they don't use fancy words or wear fine clothin' th' likes o' which make a man dream an' become uppity in his thinkin'. That's what ye did for me, lass, ye made me get uppity in me thinkin', hopin' an' wishin' for that what was beyond me station in life. I can ask ye only to forgive me."

"Forgive you?"

"I be big an' blustery an' scare people into thinkin' I'm a bully," he admitted, gently stroking the fur of her cape which was resting over the chair. "But looks do be deceivin' sometimes. Beneath th' roarin' beast there is oft times a kindly heart an' th' mind o' th' dreamer, who would really like to be uppity enough to move out o' th' way o' his lot. Fat chance o' that." He smeared the back of that thick hand over his face and inched back out of the light. "I will be goin' now. Ye've given me much to stimulate me dreams, lass—much too much. Just say it once, that ye forgive me an' I'll leave an humble man."

Joanne had been clinging to the bedpost, her hands growing moist in nervous reaction. She could barely see his silhouette as he blended into the darkness by the door. Suddenly a surge of emotion within her all but catapulted her toward him. Hands reached out as if to grope her way to the man. She had to touch him, softly stroke his face, his heart was crying so loudly she had to respond.

"Jim." A hand to his face, the other to his shoulder.

"I was wrong. You are basically a fine man." On tiptoes, she reached up to kiss his cheek. "Won't you touch me?"

"I—I dare not, lass. It is nay right."

Her hands went around him, arms circling him as she reached again to kiss—this time his lips.

Only a faint touch of his large, rough hands at her waist before he stepped back, withdrawing from her grasp. " 'Tis nay a kindness ye are doin', lass. Although I much appreciate what ye are tryin' to do, I can nay take your pity; and that is what it is. I will say good night, then, an' bid ye pleasant sleep."

Joanne heard the key turn in the door, then saw a spill of light enter the room as the man left: a dark shadow, slightly bent with humility and perhaps degradation. It saddened her. The door was pulled tightly shut. She ran to the door. "Jim!"

She did not jerk it open as she wanted to do; she did not run down the hallway after him as was her foremost desire. Her lips were still tingling from where they had touched his. Of only one thing was she certain: that she had *not* kissed the lips of a murderer.

CHAPTER EIGHTEEN

Despite her limited amount of sleep and a hung-over feeling, Joanne was wide awake early the next morning. The hotel had a dining room where she could get breakfast, but unaccompanied ladies were not allowed. She would contrive something since she believed that the intake of food was especially good for eliminating that terrible next-day feeling after imbibing too heavily of wine.

Feeling a bit overdressed for that time of the day, although she had put her jewelry into a special pouch she carried beneath her skirts, she ascended to the lobby of the hotel. At the desk she first asked to have a bellboy deliver a message to Matthew Bienville's room, saying that she was ready to leave as soon as he was; that she was desirous of returning to Merrihew Manor; and that she would be awaiting him in the dining room.

"Begging your pardon, Miss," the long-nosed, lanky

desk clerk said after the bellboy had been dispatched with the message, "but unaccompanied ladies are not permitted in the dining room." His eyes scanned her lavish costume.

"Not even if I'm expecting to meet Mr. Bienville there?" she questioned.

"Not even if you were meeting the Prince Consort himself," he replied icily.

Joanne turned away from the desk, a gnawing of hunger grinding in her solar plexus. The front door opened with a flourish and a tall man with uniquely handsome features and a prodigious profile came flouncing in. While he appeared to be nattily dressed from a distance, upon closer examination one could determine patches and occasional stitches in his garments. Still he carried himself with such aplomb that those gathered about stopped to notice him. How could Joanne forget that marvelous nose—the sort to be found on an ancient Roman coin? The name slipped her. She nonetheless interrupted his course.

"Excuse me," she said, practically bumping into the man, "but you're looking for Mrs. Lillian Harper-Sharpe, are you not?"

"Don't tell me you're Mrs. Harper-Sharpe," he said with pretentious tones, "I've known that creature since my jaded childhood. Alas!"

Joanne cast a glance toward the desk clerk who was watching her with a jaundiced eye. "I'm Joanna—Joanna Phenwick. I'm certain Mrs. Harper-Sharpe must have mentioned me to you."

The man searched his memory. The name had a vaguely familiar ring. "Ah, yes, Phenwick! The pianist person!"

"Susannah is my cousin," she explained. "You are hungry, aren't you?" She put her hand to his arm as if she wanted to take hold.

"Have you ever known an actor who wasn't always slightly famished?" he returned.

"Would you have breakfast with me?" she whispered. "Otherwise I can't go into the dining room unaccompanied."

The man eyed the desk clerk, then, with a gracious bow, he said: "I would be honored, kind lady, providing it is your treat."

The man was Jonathan Hobson, the leading man with Isaac Colton-Smith's theatrical company. The entire breakfast conversation was a recital of his dramatic experiences in the acting profession. Jonathan knew endless tales, and Joanne suspected that he made up many of them. Still it was a delightful time for her in the wonderland of make-believe known as the theatre.

Joanne had well finished breakfast and Jonathan Hobson had departed for his destination when Matthew finally put in a sleepy appearance.

"I had no idea you wanted to leave so early this morning," Matthew complained through a yawn. "I thought we would probably spend the day in London and return to Merrihew Manor late this afternoon. Never mind. I'm up and functioning now, at least as well as I intend to be this day. I shall no doubt doze all the way from London."

Moody and not well disposed after the gala evening before, Matthew was not his personable self. Easily irritated about practically anything, he chose to remain sullenly silent and pretended to doze off long before he actually did.

Joanne had evolved from her morning-after condition. While Matthew's attitude did not please her, she was understanding to a point. Yet she wanted to question him about where he had been after leaving her in the early hours of the morning. She restrained her curiosity and did not let it be known that she knew he had not been in his room.

The journey was basically uneventful in the gray, mist-filled morning. Periodically Joanne glanced at the man beside her in the carriage. Even asleep he appeared handsome. Yet there were so many questions. She was dissatisfied about his dishonest explanation for being out in the pasture the night he had spent at Merrihew Manor. A strange circumstance.

Supposing Matthew had lured Adriane from her room and made romantic overtures toward her. He had left Joanne in a desirous mood, having earlier mentioned something about "street-girls." Had his desires become so ardent that he attempted an adventure with poor, inexperienced Adriane? Had she objected, resisted? A fight perhaps. Threatened exposure. Fear. A blow far too severe for her fragile nature to tolerate.

Perhaps a similar situation had happened with Sara Cornhill at an earlier time, when Matthew was spending a night at the inn. The innkeeper might recognize him, but chances are few others in the village would. Had he gone out for a frolic, met the unwilling Sara and attempted to persuade her to the satisfaction of his wants? Rejection. Words. She would inform her brother Jim. Silence.

But what of the bloody marks at the throat where flesh appeared to be torn loose by teeth? The word vampire was practically foreign to her, except that she had recalled seeing the word in one of the occult books written by Rosea Hackleby. She puzzled it then, she puzzled it now. A dog might have bitten there: a possibility, but not likely on two persons in the identical place.

Her thoughts often strayed from the man beside her to Jim Cornhill, whom she found exciting: a man of exaggerated masculinity, still not a person without depth. Although she feared him for some unexplained reason, she admired him and felt stimulated simply by thinking of him. But other men affected her in a similar way: Jonathan Hobson, for instance, or Alister Tweedly, and, although she would not admit it to a soul, she also found a fascination in Cyrus Quigg. There were others, she thought, and realized that she was principally reacting to the physical man, not the inner self, the spiritual, the mental aspects. That could be dangerous since the physical is so transitory at best. Yet it held such a driving excitement.

Matthew stirred as the carriage turned into the drive before Merrihew Manor. He awakened with a yawn and appeared momentarily surprised to see Joanne sitting beside him. Peering out the window before he spoke, he said, "We've reached Merrihew already?"

"It takes no time at all when you're asleep."

"Forgive me. I must be terrible company. I do apologize," he stated, shaking the sleepiness from himself.

"You didn't sleep well last night?"

"As a matter of fact, I didn't," he replied, avoiding further discussion.

Nearing the mansion, the carriage slowed. Quigg appeared at the front door to help Joanne from the vehicle. He eyed her suspiciously with a controlled smirk. Her immediate impulse was to explain that the night had been spent innocently, so to speak; still she realized she owed the servant no explanation whatsoever.

"Has Miss Ornby been down for breakfast this morning?" Joanne questioned to ignore the inference in the butler's expression.

"Miss Ornby left last evening," Quigg reported. "Lord Weston insisted she spend the night at Falcon Heath Castle."

"But Lydia was given instructions to remain here," Joanne explained.

"I realize that was the plan, Miss," Quigg responded, "but she awakened after being given the powders and became restless. Mrs. Sharlock said the young lady was beside herself. She insisted upon seeing you. When she was told you were gone, she was certain something terrible had happened to you, too. That practically coincided with the appearance of Lord Weston. He comforted the distraught creature and persuaded her to go with him to Falcon Heath Castle."

"Then I must go get her at once," Joanne exclaimed. "Poor Lydia! How could I ever have been so thoughtless as to leave her alone?"

Matthew consented to accompany Joanne. Joply got fresh horses and the carriage was ready to go in a matter of moments. Less than fifteen minutes, the ride was uneventful. Joanne voiced her apprehension and concern for her cousin, swearing that she would see that Lydia was returned as quickly as possible to the United States.

They were met by a starchy butler, who showed them into the sitting room while he summoned Lady Genevieve. The old gothic castle had few livable rooms, but Lord Henry had long promised to remodel and progressively open other rooms. Still they did not entertain lavishly, rarely taking in overnight guests.

Lady Genevieve, a not altogether lovely person, arrived breezily, the ruffles of her yellow gown fluttering

as she moved. A pleasant smile was difficult for her face
but she made an effort and was almost successful.

"My dear Miss Phenwick!" the woman said with recognition. "This is an unexpected pleasure. Unfortunately
you didn't arrive earlier. Luncheon has been over only
a short time."

"Thank you, Lady Genevieve, but we're not hungry,"
Joanne returned. "We have come about Lydia. Her sister's funeral is to be this afternoon."

"Lydia?" The long nose appeared even longer and the
large eyes half-closed as she pulled her head backward
in question.

"Lydia Ornby, my cousin."

"Oh, yes." Lady Genevieve smiled in embarrassment.
"She was in a terribly depressed mood when she arrived last evening—as any of us might be under the circumstances. She was established in the guest room on
the second floor. My butler reported this morning that
she slept well and ate a bit. For some reason, I had the
notion that Miss Ornby had returned to Merrihew Manor
earlier in the day. Had I thought she was here, I would
have arranged to have her have luncheon with me. I
must apologize."

"Then perhaps she has left," Joanne stated, skeptical
about the lady's attitude. Was she feigning innocence or
did she actually not know the whereabouts of Lydia?
"You did not see her leave. Would you mind sending
your butler to examine her room? Or if that is inconvenient, Mr. Bienville and I can have a look."

"Why don't you have a look for yourself?" she said,
now with a blank, somewhat distant expression. She
gave instructions how to reach the designated room.

Lady Genevieve's attitude struck Joanne as being most
peculiar as they climbed the stairs. Matthew put his

hand to her arm as they reached the second floor; apparently he, too, sensed something unusual happening. Neither spoke until they reached the door to the chamber and knocked.

"No response," commented Matthew. He rapped a second time and the door squeaked open with the percussion of his effort. Pushing it further open, he peered in. "I don't see anyone."

Joanne stepped into the room. "Lydia?" The bed was unmade, Lydia's clothing was still draped over a chair where it had been placed the night before. A singular hush fell over the room.

Matthew paced about, examining the closet and the recesses of the room which were used as dressing areas and perhaps places for storage. The fireplace, while filled with dead ashes, gave no indication that it had been recently lit, probably not since the night before. "She's not here."

"But her clothing is here."

"There's no room to hide beneath the bed. Have you any other suggestions where I should look?"

"Don't be cross with me, Matthew. I'm deeply worried."

"I can see you are. I don't mean to appear unsympathetic."

"Perhaps we should check about in the other rooms."

"Without Lady Genevieve's permission?" asked Matthew.

"She said we might look for Lydia. Our search will simply take us beyond the prescribed room," Joanne reasoned.

Matthew laughed, catching her in his arms. "You're a wonderful little schemer, aren't you, my pretty?"

"I don't know how wonderful, Matthew, but I admit

I am somewhat of a schemer." She kissed him playfully upon the cheek, then pulled quickly away from him, clasping his hand and dragging him from the room.

For the next fifteen minutes they rummaged through the second-floor rooms, finding mostly collections of long-unused pieces of furniture. Most of the rooms seemed to have been unoccupied for years. An overall dusty feeling. Lack of light. Evidence of rodents. Destruction. Faded mementoes of past glories.

Finally as they were about to go to the first floor and report to Lady Genevieve, the sound of faint struggle came from a third-floor room. Thinking it to be a rodent, they almost dismissed it until a loud clunking sound from the same direction made them curious. The winding stairway led to a single turret room.

Swinging the door open, Joanne was startled to see her cousin reclining on a stack of large pillows used as mattresses. Her clothes were in disarray and she was partly exposed. Lord Henry had leapt back at the opening of the door and was busy trying to look unrumpled. He came nowhere close— Breeches gaping, shirtless and barefoot.

"Oh, how do you do, Miss Phenwick, Matthew? Pleasant day we're having, isn't it?" Lord Henry sputtered. "I just came up to show Miss Ornby the view from here. It's really quite interesting."

"It's strange you weren't observing the view when our carriage drove up a short while ago," countered Joanne. "Come, Lydia, that's hardly the way you should appear for your sister's funeral."

Lydia whimpered. "He forced me to come up here."

Lord Henry's eyes popped, air about to explode his cheeks. "Only to see the view."

"Never mind," Joanne said as she took her cousin's

wrist. "There's Adriane lying in her coffin, waiting to be buried, and here's you—"

"Oh, Adriane! Poor, poor Adriane!" Lydia was immediately convulsed with tears and limply clung to Joanne.

"My motives were entirely innocent!" declared Lord Henry, now with a robe about him, as he stood at the front door.

Lydia and Joanne were in the carriage, Matthew across from them.

Lady Genevieve stood at an open window nearby. She knew otherwise about her husband's motives and her expression told Joanne so.

Lord Henry waved. None of the occupants of the carriage responded as it lurched around the driveway and out to the road. Pathetically Lord Henry returned to the house, feeling beaten and angry that he had to face Lady Genevieve with a contrived explanation which neither of them would believe.

CHAPTER NINETEEN

With Matthew's assistance, Joanne got Lydia back t
Merrihew Manor and prepared for the funeral. The v
car arrived at the designated time and was impatient t
get on with the matter since he grumpily believed tha
such Christian events belonged in a parish church, not
private chapel. The affair was simple with the house
hold staff in attendance. Alister Tweedly, Toby Albrigh
Quigg and Matthew were the pallbearers. The body wa
immediately taken to the Merrihew cemetery adjoinin
the mansion and buried. Lydia wept and wanted to flin
herself into the grave atop her sister; but Joanne re
strained her.

Because he had other matters to which he had to at
tend, Matthew left Merrihew immediately after the fu
neral, assuring Joanne that he would return sometim
that evening.

Mrs. Sharlock had been instructed to pack all of Ly

dia's and Adriane's things and have them loaded onto a carriage. Toby and Alister were summoned to do the loading. Then, with Alister in the driver's seat, Joanne put her cousin into the vehicle and got in beside her.

"Where are we going?" questioned Lydia, still in her funeral attire, which was nothing more than the black dress she often wore about the house.

"I'm taking you to London," Joanne explained, "getting you a room at the Prince Edward and putting you under the watchful care of an actress friend of mine. Then I'm going instantly to the Medallion office and arrange passage for you on the first voyage to Boston or Portland. Then you will either reside with Great-aunt Jane or Cousin Rebecca. You're not to remain in England a moment beyond the time you can possibly leave."

"But what of you?" sobbed Lydia, feeling a certain relief at the plans for her future.

"I will remain at Merrihew for awhile," Joanne related, having to speak loudly over the rumble of the wheels and bracing herself with the jerky movement. "My father is due in London anytime now. I'll wait at Merrihew until that time."

"Then return to America with him?"

"I think not."

The ride was too bumpy and noisy to be conducive to easy conversation. Hence, they each turned to their private thoughts and speculations.

Lydia was deposited at the Prince Edward in a luxurious suite of rooms, far more ostentatious than she was accustomed. Bright and airy, the atmosphere would help to eradicate her gloomy attitude. Joanne further made arrangements with the hotel officials to hire a lady com-

panion to remain with her cousin for the duration of her
stay, one who was not to let her out of her sight.

A tearful departure with a promise from Joanne that
she would return to visit her frequently. Then, as she
left, Joanne thought that that would be a marvelous
excuse for her to be in London often.

Next she went to Mrs. Lillian Harper-Sharpe's room
and offered the actress a sum of cash to keep a periodic
watch on Lydia, perhaps taking her to dine on occasion.
Lillian was elated at being cast in such a well-paying
role, and she promised to do her best.

As she was leaving the Prince Edward, Joanne encountered Jonathan Hobson. He was going to join other
members of the theatrical company and invited Joanne
to go along to meet them. It was a lark. She would take
the time, ordering Alister Tweedly to meet her with the
carriage at the theatre in forty-five minutes. En route, she
mentioned that Lydia had temporarily taken up resi-
dence at the Prince Edward and suggested that Hobson
might care to visit her since she would have a great deal
of time on her hands. Again there was an offering of
money.

Her experience with the dramatic troupe was one Joanne would long remember. She felt an immediate rapport with each of the pretenders; and they brought out
a certain eccentricity of character in herself. The way
she laughed and conversed, none of the thespians would
have guessed she had recently come from a funeral. Before the visit was over, she promised that she would
come and apprentice with them once her cousin Susannah returned from her concert tour—perhaps before, if
she definitely left Merrihew Manor and moved to London.

Fifteen minutes later than she had promised, she met

Alister. She was easily forgiven. The groom enjoyed watching people and he had had his eyes full that afternoon.

One final stop before they returned to the country. The carriage was directed to the Medallion office. Lex had previously introduced Joanne to the persons in charge of the establishment, and they recognized her instantly as a Phenwick, spying a remarkable resemblance between her and her father.

At Medallion she made arrangements for Lydia to have passage on a ship leaving in two weeks for Portland—a lucky break—which would be the same Joanne's father would be arriving on. Peter would be going to Elton School to visit his sons and Joanne would go with him. Perhaps she could persuade him to take her to the continent to hear Susannah play.

Late afternoon before Joanne arrived back at Merrihew Manor, where she was surprised to find R. Piedmont Stopp, Constable Sedley Jones and Lord Henry Weston waiting for her. The carriage was sent back to the stable and she was given a few minutes to freshen herself before she joined the men.

Quigg had served tea and brought in a fresh pot as Joanne arrived in the library. The butler furtively viewed the men and stared obediently at Joanne before he left.

"A queer fellow that," Constable Jones commented, indicating the direction Quigg left. "Can't place me finger on it, but he simply looks out of place in that satin butler's outfit. He's got the body of a laborer, all distorted and bulky with muscles." He patted his flabby belly self-consciously.

"Perhaps he has not always been a butler," Lord Henry suggested, avoiding eye contact with Joanne.

"Well, whatever—" Piedmont Stopp said and waved

his hand in a sign that he wished to change the subject. "We three have recently returned from the Cornhill's place."

"Jim?" Joanne asked before catching herself.

"No, Jim Cornhill was not there. Nor had he been there since yesterday," Piedmont stated. "We had a man watching the house. I suspect the man is in hiding. In the meantime we were able to acquire one of Jim's old shoes and matched them to the footprints found in the pasture. There is no mistaking that they're a match all right."

"It is our suggestion, Miss Phenwick," Constable Jones remarked, "that it would be best for you not to remain at Merrihew alone."

"With a house full of servants," Joanne rejoined, "and Matthew Bienville, I don't see how you could think that I would be alone."

"Bienville?" questioned Stopp. "Has he moved in on a permanent basis?"

She started to flare up with a response, then controlled herself. "He is a guest here."

"You would surely be welcome to stay at Falcon Heath Castle," Lord Henry said, almost without thinking.

The expression she flashed told him what she thought. "As you observed, Quigg is husky enough. I will feel protected with him about. Then there's Tweedly and Albright."

"All three of these men were no protectors for Sara Cornhill nor your cousin Miss Ornby," commented Lord Henry.

"And speaking of Bienville, which we were only a moment ago," interjected Piedmont Stopp, "we spoke to him a short while before you arrived. He seems greatly preoccupied with missions that take him hither and yon, indicating that he would only be present at this domain at periodic intervals."

With adequate warnings to Joanne, the three men left. In parting, Lord Henry admonished Quigg to take special care of Joanne and to keep a protective eye on her. Their carriage rumbled noisily away.

Quigg watched as Joanne moved into the house and asked if there was any more she wished of him for the time being. She said there was nothing. He quietly disappeared as if on little cat's paws. When she turned about, he was gone.

A shiver as she stared down the long, shadowy hallway. Dark at the top of the stairs on the second floor. Draperies had been pulled over the windows to shut out strong afternoon light and had not been pulled back. Suddenly the appearance of feet and legs descending the stairs, finally the handsome face of Matthew. As usual he was dressed immaculately, which did not indicate his present mode nor destination.

"Well, well, have they gone?" asked he as he came up to where she was standing.

She ran to him, lips begging to be kissed. Nodding, she let her arms feel the security of being about him.

"I suspect they're onto something," he commented. "Excuse me, there's a thing or two I left in the library."

She went with him, still touching, holding as much as she could. "Are you disturbed about something?"

"Disturbed?" He chuckled artificially. "Whatever gave you such a notion?"

"Your attitude."

"My attitude is no different than usual," he returned with a deceptive smile. Hand to his forehead. "I'm still feeling a bit of the effects from last night, my dear, so perhaps I am off my ordinary demeanor."

"Perhaps that is it." She held her face to be kissed again.

"You're in a strange mood yourself this afternoon."

"Because I want to be kissed?"

"I suspect you feel safe," he said playfully, "because you know I am preoccupied and won't want to carry the meaning of a kiss to its ultimate conclusion. I'm often passionate in the afternoon—not this one in particular."

"No. I want to be kissed and held because I need reassurance."

"Reassurance? About what? That I did not kill your cousin?"

"That wasn't in my mind."

"Wasn't it, my precious?" Matthew snapped. "Oh, yes, my dear, I can tell what is worrying you. You're afraid you might be falling in love with a murderer—a murderer of your own cousin—and you want to resist before it's too late."

"Aren't you being terribly presumptive to think I might be falling in love with you?" she fired.

"Am I?"

Pause. Quivering lips. Her eyes stared intensely into his. An instant later his arms were wrapped about her and she was pulled tightly to him. Lips touched, pressed, seemed to melt into each other. Flames of excitement. Electric tingling. Momentarily uncontrolled passion. A moment of happening. Of consent? Of rejection? Something happened, as though a candle had quickly been snuffed out, and the energy ceased to flow from one to the other.

"I have to go, Joanne. I'm late as it is."

Her hands fell limply. Lips stinging. Emotions raw. Quietly. "Then go. You *will* be back later?"

"Yes, my dear." Another quick embrace as she stood

without responding, then he quickly dashed from the room. The door clicked closed behind him.

Joanne was trembling. She had grown icy cold. A spear of pain, jabbing, jabbing, jabbing. To the window, she could see the carriage pulling down the drive, Joply in the driver's seat. Instead of turning in the direction of the village and ultimately London, the carriage took the opposite direction and disappeared into the forest.

Emptiness. Still she knew the man would return. He would be less preoccupied and perhaps more romantic. She must think of something else. *Anything* else.

Near the door, she saw a folded piece of paper, obviously a letter. Picking it up, she opened and read it. From a solicitor, it dealt with the information that there were claimants from among the poorer classes who believed that they were legitimate heirs to the Merrihew estate. And as a matter of fact, one such man has begun procedures to investigate the legality of his claim. Because it was stiffly worded in formal terms and professional jargon, she did not fully comprehend the contents. Still she deduced that there was an individual who was attempting to get a share of the estate which had become exclusively that of the Phenwicks. Was that individual Matthew Bienville? Was he involved in some sort of treachery to get the property which he believed to be his? She had no notion how a situation like that would work, nor how it could be resolved. She only knew that she had even more of a suspicious attitude toward the man for whom she felt such strong romantic inclinations.

The door to the library suddenly opened with a defiant jerk. She turned to see the startled expression of Quigg as he came to gather the tea things. Regaining his composure, the butler went directly to collect the cups and saucers.

"Excuse me, Miss Phenwick. I came for the things." Now a relaxed attitude as he did his work.

She studied him as she pretended to be occupied with a book into which she had shoved the letter.

The man was without his uniform coat, wearing a tight vest and knee breeches. Again she was aware of his somewhat chunky, although nicely proportioned build. She recalled the observation of Constable Jones. Without his coat, his musculature was more remarkably defined and accentuated.

"You were observing me, Miss Phenwick?" he asked as he suddenly turned around to face her. Penetrating eyes. A salacious smile. A self-conscious strutting of his physique as if he were purposefully putting himself on display.

"I—that is—only in passing." Her throat was dry.

"It was not the first time I have been aware of your scrutiny, Miss Phenwick," he said. "Is there something about me that bothers you?"

"No. I think you are a fine, efficient butler. You handle your position well," she stammered.

"My position—as a butler? Yes, I take great effort to see that I do my job well," he stated.

She had a desire to put the desk between them. As she moved, her legs felt wobbly. "Have you always occupied such a position?"

"Here at Merrihew I have," he returned, stacking things on the tray. "But I have known periods of hard labor, especially in my youth. That is why I have become so muscular."

"Muscular?"

"Hadn't you observed?"

Joanne swallowed. "Well, as a matter of fact—"

"You have?"

"Yes." She was flustered. "That was why I happened to ask—"

"About my position?"

"Yes." She was abundantly aware of the sensuality of the man, the sheer magnetic attraction that oozed from him. "You speak well. Are you educated?"

"Mostly self-educated, Miss. I have always felt unfulfilled, thwarted by poverty and the menial positions I had to hold," he explained. "I regret not having been born into a better class. I cannot help that. I have educated myself well, Miss Phenwick, in many and various aspects of life. Haven't you noticed I have a hypnotic way about me? My eyes are fierce and compelling, are they not?"

She glanced, then looked away. "Yes, they are."

He chuckled lightly, sardonically, as he lifted the tray and prepared to leave the room. "There have been ladies who have found my eyes irresistible."

And the rest of you, too, no doubt, she thought. "You may be excused, Quigg. I'm certain you have other activities to pursue."

"That I have, Miss," he said, and his attitude was almost impudent. "If there's anything more I can do for you, please let me know." He started out, then stopped. "Will you be dining alone?"

"Alone?" The word had an eerie impact, thundering through her. "I—no—I should imagine Mr. Bienville will return in time for supper."

Quigg smiled, his eyes bouncing up and down. "I should imagine." He silently left the room.

Alone. A horrible sinking feeling came over her. "Please, God, let Matthew return in time for supper."

CHAPTER TWENTY

The sun was descending, aiming toward a distant line of treetops. Gray clouds made dark shadows on the horizon, long, narrow lines. Still yellow, the sun was evolving into shades of gold, soon orange. Joanne stared from the window of her room. She had halfheartedly lighted a fire, but got mostly smoke. Instead of ringing for Quigg and having to endure another encounter with the man she was coming to consider more and more sensual, she donned heavier clothing and wrapped a wollen shawl about her shoulders.

Moist-eyed, she gazed strangely into the sunset. A premonition that something unusual was going to happen. A fear of the coming night and being alone in the old house. For all her spoken faith in the servants, doubt fell about her like a curtain. What was the sensation? Why the apprehension?

In the distance she heard a clock bonging the hour.

She counted the strokes and calculated that there was a good hour, perhaps longer, before nightfall. What she needed to quell that nervousness was exercise. Run up and down the stairs? No, the household staff would think she had lost her good sense. Walk? Perhaps outside with the dogs. Still that would be slow and plodding. A ride? Why not? Yes. That had become one of her favorite means of exercise and she was now an expert with a horse.

Appropriately dressed, she hurried to the stable, passing Mrs. Sharlock in the process and announcing that she would be out for an hour or so and that supper was to be at the usual time. Alister Tweedly was surprised to see Joanne approaching the stable. Usually that time of night he and Toby Albright prepared to eat and then lazed about during the evening hours. When she strode toward the stable, the men knew there would be some alteration in their customary schedule. Toby appeared as Joanne reached Alister and gave commands that she wanted a horse saddled.

"Tell me, Toby Albright," Joanne questioned as Alister went to tend to the mount, "what do you think of the murders that have occurred here?"

"I confess they do give me th' jitters, they do," the stableman replied, his country face looking more mundane than usual. "I confess, also, that I do sleep close along side o' Alister, I do. If'n he moves, me eyes pop open like that an' I reach for a knife what I keeps by th' bed."

"Do you have any notion who might have committed such crimes?"

"Nay, lass, I don't." He sniffed noisily. "Some say as how it were Jim Cornhill, but I can nay say."

"Ye can nay say *what*, Toby?" asked Alister as he appeared with the horse.

" 'Bout Jim Cornhill bein' th' one what murdered them girls."

"Nay, it was nay Jim," Alister said. "Jim an' me we grew up together. Jim an' me we done a lot o' things together. I'd trust Jim like he was me own brother."

"Was Jim Cornhill fond of his sister?" asked Joanne.

"Jim is one who looked after his family when there was no one else to do it," Alister explained. "That ol' lady, she ain't much good with them—nay like Jim. He were father and mother and big brother all rolled into one. A good heart has Jim."

Alister helped Joanne into the saddle. She hoisted her skirts and rode astride, which she preferred.

"Would ye want me to go along, Miss?" questioned Alister.

"No, thank you, Alister. I prefer to be with my thoughts." The horse pranced, stepping nervously until she calmed him. "One other question. Have you both been in service here as long as Cyrus Quigg has been?"

"Nay, I were a lad when Quigg began here," Alister informed, curiously twisting his head in an unspoken question. "I was a lad in th' village. Quigg, when he was younger, used to box on the common with any sport what would take him on. Pretty soon he ran outa lads what were sports, an' that was the last I ever saw him box."

"You mean a pugilist?"

"I can nay say since I do nay know th' word."

"Oh dear, I would have never thought that of Mr. Quigg," Joanne stated. "Yet on the other hand—"

"I seen a strong man down in London once," Toby interjected excitedly, "who had muscles like I ne'er seen before. Quigg, he was th' next strongest—least ways that is how it seemed when I was a lad."

Yes, she knew he was a powerfully constructed individual, but she could only guess as to what extent he was developed. The thought made her flush with light embarrassment. She motioned for Alister to lead the horse out.

The roan gelding was an anxious beast, desirous of stretching his fine legs. Fast. Strong-willed. To ride him was an experience and a challenge which Joanne readily accepted. Generally she proved to be his mistress and he respected her for it. However, there were times when she thought perhaps he might have a vengeful streak mixed with his obstinacy. She indicated the direction she wanted to go, and they went that way—for awhile. Up ahead, where the road forked, Joanne intended to go to the right where the way was familiar to her; the gelding, who was called Jack, decided he wanted to go to the left. No matter how fiercely she commanded, the animal refused to alter his direction, nor to obey. He was determined to go his way and he did.

Within ten minutes, the surrounding countryside became unfamiliar to her. Still the horse refused to heed her demands. Now into a forested area, where heavy shadows were hanging like drifts of gloom. Panic! She yanked on the reins as hard as she could. Nothing. She yelled at him, but the animal was deaf to her words. As she flew past a thick grove of pines, she had the sensation that she had attracted someone's attention and that they were following her. She dared not look back. Her hands felt as if they were becoming raw from the cutting leather as she gripped the reins. Low-hanging limbs. Twigs slapped her stingingly in the face. Her only hope was that the forest would get so thick that it would slow Jack if not bring him to a halt.

With no evident provocation, Jack suddenly slowed and in moments had come to a complete halt. Joanne slid off the beast and stoutly secured the reins to a tree trunk. She needed time to get her bearings, to rub sore places and perhaps to find a brook for water. After the heavy breathing and snorting of the horse had subsided, and her own pulse weakened, she perceived the sound of running water. Scouting forward, she pushed her way through the slapping limbs. Three long drinks of the refreshing liquid, she was ready to go back and escort Jack to the trickling brook.

A light tap on the shoulder, and she automatically turned about to find herself suddenly caught in a bear hug; two strong arms about her waist and her body pulled tightly to that of Jim Cornhill. She struggled fruitlessly since he had a powerful advantage over her.

"Jim Cornhill! Put me down this instant!"

"Scream all ye like, me pretty thing, no one'll hear ye in these woods, 'ceptin' th' forest creatures." He laughed merrily, the scent of wine on his breath. In a moment he had plunged his face toward hers, thick lips touched and kissed lavishly about her face. His whiskers were a stubble of discomfort, still his very presence created a disconcerting excitement. She wanted to kiss him back, to respond as she had never done before with any man. She giggled, her torso writhing as if to escape his arms and yet not really wanting to.

When she wiggled her arms free, she threw them about his neck and kissed him almost as violently as he had kissed her. Whiskers scratched her lips and made them all the more sparkle with excitement.

"Truce! Truce, lass! Ye're a wild one when ye come

unloose, ain't ye?" he exclaimed as he put her to the ground and wiped his mouth with the back of his wrist. Taking a wineskin from his waist, he offered it first to her, then took a swig himself. "What th' very devil do ye be doin' out in these woods this time o' th' day?"

She lunged forward to kiss him again, nearly knocking him off balance.

"Ay, ye are a playful lass this evenin', aren't ye?" he shouted, catching his wineskin in time to keep from losing the contents. "Ye be careful or ye're liable to get a wee bit more o' a romp than ye had in mind. An', while I confess I am o' a mind to take ye to sport, I also confess I have too much respect for ye to impose me wishes unduly on ye."

"What if they're my wishes as well?" she said teasingly.

"Are they?"

She thought a moment. "No. They might be in my thoughts, but completely against my better judgment."

"Do ye have better judgment at a time like this, lass?"

"I try, Jim. . . . I try." She put her hands to him and held her mouth to be kissed again.

" 'Tis nay right to do this!" Jim said several minutes later as he turned from her. "Me mind must be single-goaled. I can nay be distracted from findin' me sister's murderer."

Joanne went up behind him and lightly caressed his strong back. "I never took you for being such a sentimental person."

"Don't let th' bulk fool ye, lass." Again his hand swiped over his face and he sniffed deeply. "Cum, lass, I'll show ye somethin'."

"Show me what? It's nearly dark."

"Ay, an' it is in th' first hours o' darkness they begin their weird games."

"They? Games?"

"Cum, ye'll see."

She grabbed hold of his sleeve, detaining him. "Wait, Jim. There is a question I must ask you."

"Can it nay wait?"

"It can, but I would rather it didn't."

Jim turned to stare into the face that darkness was quickly obscuring. "Ask."

"Your farm, the Cornhill property is fairly close to the Merrihew estate," she began.

"Ay, that it is."

"Have your people been long on that land?"

"For generations. Me father says it was over two hundred years. Perhaps it was longer than that."

"Two hundred years? Are you wealthy people?"

Jim laughed cynically. "That do be a foolish question, lass. We barely scrape for a livin', we do."

"Is there any possibility that you might in some way be related to the Merrihew family?"

"Th' *what?*" Laughter. "Nay, lass, we Cornhills have been th' servants to th' Merrihews, but there is nay legitimate Merrihew blood in our veins."

"And illegitimate?"

"Ay, that no one can say for certain, life bein' what it is."

"Then you would have no reason to think you were related to the Merrihew family?"

Again the ridiculing laughter. "I nay know what ye are gettin' at, lass, but it is gettin' funnier and funnier. Or should I say, sillier and sillier."

Joanne kissed him again, lightly, compassionately and permitted him to hold her hand as they walked back to where Jack was waiting.

"Now then, what is it you want me to observe?"

"Ye'll see."

Jim's horse was tied a distance from Jack. Soon they were back on the path and riding into the darkness of night. Silver light brightened the sky as a full moon rose over the trees.

"How much further is it?" Joanne called over the rumble of horses' hooves.

"Beyond yonder hill," Jim pointed as he shouted.

As they reached the summit, Jim motioned for them to slow to a halt. The place was barren with only a few straggly bushes.

"Why've we dismounted here?" Joanne questioned.

"Because if'n we rode any further, we might be heard."

They crept forward, that earlier feeling of apprehension running through Joanne again. She remained close to Jim, often touching as they stealthily moved up the hill.

A campfire was being built and people were mingling around it. Strange chanting. Soon the random movement evolved into primitive dancing, sensual swaying of bodies and lewd gyrations. Jim put his arm about her to give support.

"What is it?" Joanne asked.

" 'Tis a cult. They do be practicin' magic."

"Magic? Supernatural?"

"Ay, lass, I do believe that is part o' it."

As the communicants of that singular ritual danced themselves into a frenzy, their chant became louder and they were soon in the process of divesting themselves of their clothing. Soon flabby naked bodies were reeling suggestively about the fire, the crimson flames reflecting off their flesh.

In the midst of the excitement, a bull-like male creature came bounding out from the shrubbery. The headdress he wore was indistinguishable from where Joanne and Jim were standing, but the firelight caught the strong muscular definition of his body. The sight was both disgusting and exciting. Joanne clung to Jim and wanted to be held protectively as she reacted to the sheer lasciviousness of the spectacle.

The bull-like creature danced frantically, taking first one and then another partner from the congregation as his perverted enthusiasm appeared to be increasing. His strength attracted and repelled without discrimination.

A chicken let out a piercing squawk and Jim quickly shielded Joanne's eyes and all but carried her away back down the hill.

"What was about to happen?"

"Th' sacrifice, lass. 'Twas only a chicken, but 'twould nay be a pleasant sight. Cum, ye've seen enough."

"Sacrifice?"

"Only dumb animals are put upon their altar," Jim informed. "Never human sacrifice, if'n that be what ye were thinkin'."

"I should hope not," she said as they reached the horses. "Why did you bring me to see this?"

"So ye might understand some things, lass, about this country. Those people ye saw naked in th' ruddy moonlight," he explained, "they do be th' good people who live hereabouts. O' a Sunday, ye'll see them prayin' an' hymn-singin' in th' regular church pews. But there do be somethin' perverse 'bout human nature what makes 'em want to delve into th' bizarre an' supernatural. I nay can answer ye why that is. I will tell ye this: I found me sister Sara down there one night flippin' about in her nothin'-at-all."

"Do you think those people had something to do with her death—and subsequently with Adriane's?"

"I nay be certain, but I do have me suspicions," Jim related. "I would like to get me hands on that big fellow what cum dancin' out with th' big thing on his head."

"What makes you suspect these people?"

"When your cousin was found in th' outline o' stones where me sister was layin', then I began to put two an' two together," Jim explained. "I nay may be right, but I must see it out. Cum with me once more, then I'll see ye're taken back to Merrihew Manor."

"Where now?"

"Ye'll see."

CHAPTER TWENTY-ONE

They rode in silence for less than a mile from the place they had observed the weird rites. Assorted questions presented themselves to Joanne's mind, questions she doubted Jim could answer. She wished she had spent more time delving through Rosea Hackleby's books about the occult. The only account that truly had fascinated her in those volumes concerned the spirit possession of her Cousin Rachel—a person who had been killed by her possessors long before Joanne was born. Still it was such a bizarre story, that it had remained prominent in her imagination. Upon asking old Rosea about it, the woman went into great detail about the witch trials in Salem, Massachusetts. Rosea's theory was that the spirits of two disincarnate witches who had been burned at the stake, after all those years, had found the susceptible body of Rachel and had invaded it. Rosea tried to explain to Joanne and her brothers, but the notion was so extraordinary that it was difficult to fathom. Yet some of the rituals she had found recorded in the old books were similar to the one she had witnessed that night.

The cottage was made of mud and rocks, the roof thatched with several layers of straw and enough soil that each spring a fresh crop of weeds grew upon it. Over the years it had built up certain resistance to the weather. One large room and a small storage room. A stone fireplace. Earthen floors covered with braided rags pieced together to make a covering. A small table. Two wee benches. A large, somewhat comfortable chair. A bed of goose feather mattresses. No windows. A collection of odors from as long as odors persist. The other scents disguised by the overpowering fragrance of a combination of potent spices. A black cat roamed mysteriously about the small room as if protecting his domain. A hand-made broom resting at the hearth.

"Helen Goodlay, do ye be home?" Jim questioned as the weight of his hand upon the door caused it to swing open. He peered in under the low door. "Helen Goodlay!"

The old woman appeared a gnarled shadow coming around the side of the building, three pieces of cut-up wood in her hand. A scarf tied about her head, an old shawl around her shoulders. Bent considerably forward, she seemed to be diligently searching for some article on the ground. She could not rear her head back and could only observe the visitors by raising her eyes as far as they would go in her head. A large nose and a sharp chin. Toothless. Cheeks sunken. Hands so knotted they looed like deformed talons.

A raspy, whispery voice asked, "What do ye want? Who do ye be?"

"'Tis me, Jim Cornhill, Miss Goodlay."

"Ay. So 'tis. Who's she?"

"This is Miss Phenwick from Merrihew Manor."

"Merrihew Manor?" The old crone cackled. "Ye'll find me palace ain't as fancy as thine, lass." She beckoned for them to enter.

In her stooped condition, it took no effort whatsoever for Helen Goodlay to enter the cottage; both Joanne and Jim had to bend down because of the low door. A tiny candle was burning on the table. The old woman went immediately to light a fire, the kindling of which had been earlier laid. While that was occurring, Jim went out back and gathered an armload of sticks for the woman, which greatly pleased her. Joanne watched, rigid as she sat on the bench. She found the combination of odors offensive and twice she sneezed with the heavy spice. Helen Goodlay chuckled in response.

With sufficient light from the fireplace, Helen waddled back to where the girl was seated. Holding gnarled fingers to her chin, Helen studied her. When Jim arrived with the wood and stacked it beside the hearth, she motioned for him to pull the comfortable chair up to the table for her to sit in. Then she motioned for him to sit on the other small bench. The candlelight played strange patterns over their faces, creating a mysterious attitude.

"Now then, why do ye be here?" asked Helen, still studying the faces before her.

Jim explained first about Adriane's murder, since he had already consulted with the old woman about that of his sister. Then he told of taking Joanne to watch the naked ritual from a distance.

Helen cackled. "Ye've never seen th' likes o' that, ha' ye, lass?"

"No, but I've read about many mysterious things," Joanne returned, wishing she had actually spent more time with Rosea Hackleby's books. She then informed them about the books, much to the old woman's curiosity.

A happy expression. "One day I should like to see such books," Helen remarked. "I would nay doubt ha' a thin' or two to add meself. Then ye must recognize that those communicants in th' vale were preparin' themselves for a magic ritual."

"Magic?"

"Ay, they do be conjurin' up somethin' or other," she said.

"Conjuring?"

"Some o' them take it seriously, but to others it do just be a means o' amusin' themselves," she continued. "Tearin' off their clothes an' dancin' about in th' moonlight can bring a bit o' unfettered joy. 'Twill end in a debauchery, nay doubt. But what else ha' they to do? 'Tis th' only merriment for poor people." She cackled again.

Jim nudged Joanne and chuckled along. Joanne smiled, but it made her feel uneasy. An apprehensive sensation was coming over her as if being in that cottage was not the thing she should be doing at that time. Also she was afraid to let her guard down and allow too great a familiarity with Jim for fear he might construe her attitude to mean consent.

Jim sensed her concern. "Actually, Miss Goodlay, 'twas some divinin' we was wantin' from ye."

"Divinin'?".

Jim explained he wanted information about the two murders and the evidence indicating vampires that was found.

"Ha' ye nay got a bit o' somethin' belongin' to each o' th' dead lasses?" asked the old woman.

Joanne shrugged.

"I have a bonnet belongin' to me sister," Jim announced, producing the starchless item and another, "along with a handkerchief belongin' to th' other one."

"How did you get Adriane's handkerchief?" Joanne demanded to know. She snatched it from him to ascertain that it was indeed her cousin's. Recognizing the embroidered initial, she handed it back.

"I have me ways o' procurin' such things, Joanne. 'Tis nay important how."

"It might be if Adriane had the handkerchief in her possession at the time she was killed."

"I swear to ye that it were not." He handed the two items to Helen Goodlay.

The old fingers soothed over the garments before she took one in each hand and held them in her lap. She closed her eyes for several minutes, breathing deeply with longer and longer periods between each inhale and exhale. Finally her watery gray eyes opened and she glanced first at one and then the other.

"Ay, 'twas th' same person what killed them both," she stated, a hazy look in her eyes. "Those were nay th' mark o' a vampire—th' likes o' which don't be in this part o' th' world—but were made to look like th' mark o' a vampire to place ye off th' scent."

"Can ye tell us somewhat more about how they happened?"

"Ay. 'Twas th' flirtatious ways o' your sister what got her in trouble, Jim. She long was nay a virgin. An' ye know yourself she oft went to th' magic ritual for a bit o' a frolic. Th' other were killed in a like way to make it appear as if ye had killed th' second in revenge for your sister's death, Jim. But, rest assured, both lasses were killed by th' same man."

"Man?"

"Ay. Had ye investigated your cousin's body carefully, ye would ha' found evidence about what I be sayin'."

Joanne had many questions as they left that cottage with the thatched roof and went to where they had left the horses.

"I think all we got was a funny old lady's opinions," Joanne stated.

"I have reason to believe she knows o' what she speaks," Jim returned, impulsively reaching for her hand and wrapping his about it. "I've gone many times to Miss Goodlay, an' she has told me th' facts about certain things what I proved to be true later. If she says there be no vampires about, then I believe."

"I didn't think much of the vampire theory to begin with," Joanne commented, her attention transferred to the electric current throbbing in her hand as a result of his touch.

Jim helped her onto the horse. His hands lingering, slipping gently as he brought them down. The disengaging of his touch made her want to extend her leg to reestablish contact. But Jim was quickly astride his mount. Moonlight. Silvery-white, so bright that one could almost see color. Her eyes swept over the man and down to his boots. Leather wet, they glistened in the moonlight. For the first time she was aware of how large they actually were. Still, for his overall proportions, they hardly seemed too big. They kicked, the horse moved. She did the same.

Heavy shadows as they rode through the forest, at times almost obscuring Jim, who had taken the lead. Joanne urged her horse to keep up with him. Then areas where the moonlight bathed them. As she kept up, she admired the stature of the man, the nobility of his carriage, straight, tall. The animal was as proud as the man who rode him.

Back into a thickness of trees. Limbs whipped occasionally. Little moonlight filtered through the branches. Jim slowed and came to a stop at the side of a rushing stream of water. Dismounting, he led his horse to drink. Joanne slid down and allowed her horse to stand beside the other.

"Ye're nay more than two kilometers from Merrihew Manor, lass," Jim explained in an offhanded manner. "Ye can find your way from here. I've other things to do."

"Tie the horses."

"Here now, what have ye in mind?" he asked without showing alarm. "I can nay dally much longer."

"Only a few moments, Jim."

"What do ye be thinkin' about? Them people dancin' 'round naked in th' magic ritual, an' th' big man with his bloody head covered?" Jim asked, teasingly.

"Not right at this moment," she replied, "but I confess I have given him some thought."

"Him? Nay all o' them?"

"Yes, all of them, too."

The horses tied, they strolled a short distance into the moonlight.

"Lassie, there do be somethin' I should tell ye," Jim said after a few seconds of silence. "That man ye was in London with th' other night, th' one what took ye to th' theatre."

"Matthew?"

"Matthew, is it?"

"Matthew Bienville."

"I wonder if ye were to see him as undressed as th'

man with th' thin' upon his head," Jim speculated, "if'n he might not strongly resemble that same man."

"What are you getting at?" she questioned suspiciously.

"When I first saw that man with ye, I knew it weren't th' first time I had ever seen him," Jim informed. "Then I recalled where it was what I did see him—an', unless I be greatly mistaken, it was at one o' them magic rituals."

"Matthew? Impossible. He wouldn't—"

"Wouldn't he, lass? I wonder," Jim said. "Where is he this night?"

"He went off—on—he said—business . . ."

Soft laughter from Jim. "An' now I have business what I must be about, lass. 'Tis gettin' late, an' there's much to do."

"Wait one moment, Jim. Please."

Jim had started to walk away. He paused, turned back. Before he could speak the question, she had leapt to him with enough force to knock him off balance. Her arms were quickly about him and she was pressed as tightly as she could get.

"Hold me for a moment, Jim," she ordered. "I want to feel your embrace."

"Give us a kiss then?"

Exotic emotional reaction, especially on the part of Joanne, was difficult to rationalize. She knew this man was not Matthew, but he was a man who intrigued her. His occasional touch had delighted her; but allowing this complete moment of contact gave her different ideas about the man.

Several minutes later, when both had forced the passion to subside, and identified it as animal attraction, Jim suggested it was time they each go their way. No matter how she inspired him, he had to control such desires as were awakened, and tend to another very important matter.

Jim rode away first at her suggestion, quickly fading into the dark forest. She questioned her feelings, her reactions, her interest in that particular man. Wanting more, she would race her steed back to Merrihew Manor and hope to exercise away at least part of her frustrations.

CHAPTER TWENTY-TWO

During practically the entire ride from the forest to Merrihew Manor, Joanne was lit by moonlight. By the time she reached the stable, the moon was high in the sky. Dogs barked at her entrance. Only Jaspar came to greet her, tail flapping and tongue dripping out the side of his mouth.

The stable was dark. She called for Toby, but received no reply. Then she shouted Alister's name. Still nothing. A post outside for tying horses, to which she fastened Jack.

A curious sensation came over her. It was not like both Alister and Toby to be away at the same time so early in the evening.

She had lost track of the time. Perhaps it was later than she suspected it to be. Curiously she stepped inside the stable. Smell of horses. Scampering of mice. Enough moonlight penetrated through the open door that she

219

could see her way to the room where Alister and Toby slept. Knocking, she waited, then knocked again. No answer. The door swung open at her touch to reveal an unoccupied room. Strange.

A thought struck her. She found a candle and matches. With a sliver of light, she made her way to the place where the carriages were kept. Matthew's carriage was not there. She started to go beyond to check the horses, but her candle went out. Groping in the darkness, she retraced her steps as best she could.

Ultimately outside, but not without receiving a small bruise in the process, she decided to leave the horse where he was tied. Surely Toby or Alister would return before long.

Jaspar lapped at her hand. He had remained outside the stable as all the dogs were trained to do.

An eeriness in the air. She could feel it as if it were something tangible. Something was wrong. Why did she have a strong compulsion to go back toward the pasture? Why that sudden curiosity?

Fortunately Jaspar accompanied her, tail wagging, as she made her way over the dampish soil to the place outlined in rocks where the bodies had been found. The footprints were still visible. What if they actually were Jim's footprints? She could not believe that he was a killer. Even if she had not become so excited by him, she found that he was basically of a tender nature, one who acted out of compassion not revenge. Yet, supposing he had taken revenge against the killer of Sara Cornhill? If Helen Goodlay was right—and Joanne put little faith in such things—Jim would not have killed out of revenge. He would have had to have had a strong motive indeed.

She stared at the outline of light, almost white, stones.

Jim admitted he had seen his sister dancing in the magic ritual. Had that perhaps provoked him sufficiently that he had had words with Sara and perhaps had gotten into a physical conflict? Suppose he accidentally killed her, then tried to cover that fact by carrying her body into the Merrihew pasture. No, that was too far fetched. Besides, if the second murder were out of revenge, why was Adriane chosen as victim?

The questions mixed with an electrical excitement in the air. Excitement of apprehension with overtones of terror. Why did she think this? Now an urgency to escape from the pasture as if she felt that someone were watching her. Perhaps they were. Lifting her skirts, she ran as rapidly as she could back to the stable.

Was someone out in that darkness, perhaps hiding in the shadows? There might as well have been, if there was not, because of her terrified reaction.

Now the distance from the stable to the house. Jaspar was at her heels. She hastened to the rear door. It was locked. Then she went to the side carriage entrance. Fortunately the door opened as she turned the knob. Jaspar remained outside, although she was very tempted to invite him in.

No light in the hallways. She made her way to the library and there found a candle. Gloom spread about that old room with the rows of books. The large clock monotonously ticked the seconds. Nine o'clock? Was it possible she had been away so long? Thinking back, she recalled they had watched the ritual for quite awhile, and that they had visited with Helen Goodlay probably close to an hour. Then there was all that riding time, and the time in the woods, and walking . . . and . . . Oh, she hoped Jim Cornhill was not the culprit behind the murders; she liked him too much.

Admitting her feeling for Jim, she had also to consider her attitude toward Matthew. If she did not have doubts about that man, she might believe that she liked him very much. But there were those doubts, discrepancies in his remarks, mysterious comings and goings through the night. And there was Jim's suspicions that Matthew had been seen at the magic ritual and insinuations that he himself might be the leader. Why did the word warlock come to her? Had she actually witnessed a witch's coven? If so, not only might Matthew be involved, but also Jim. She had to put such demoralizing thoughts from her mind.

She left the library, the candle trembling in her hand. The dark at the head of the stairs was foreboding. Go to the kitchen, perhaps find one of the servants. Get more light!

Flames were still dancing at the fire, and water was steaming in the kettle along side. Fixing herself a cup of tea, she sat in the warm kitchen. Remembering she had not eaten, she found an apple and ate it with her tea. That was sufficient for her, leaving her with a full feeling. She made a second cup of tea, hoping that someone might chance into the kitchen. Even Mrs. Sharlock would be a grim but welcomed person.

Easily nine thirty or a quarter to ten, Joanne decided that she would make a desperate run for the stairs and her room, where she would lock herself in for the night. That decided upon, the next step was to gain the courage. She had thought about both Matthew and Jim until she dared not think anymore. Thoughts were too confusing and there was no separating fiction from fact. Her reasonable, rational mind told her if it were a choice between the two, Matthew would have to be the one: he would be acceptable to her way of life and the

society in which she circulated, or would circulate in the
future. While Jim was just a lovable person with the
misfortune of having been born in the lower class and
without incentive or motivation to raise his standard of
living. Only a man of ambition could keep up with
Joanne.

The hallway was so black that the tiny candle she
carried was barely enough to create anything but a
speck of light. She might as well walk blindly through
the hall and hope her eyesight would adjust to the darkness. A moment later a draft of air came sailing through
and eliminated her decision about the candle. Now in
complete darkness she went toward the direction of the
stairway, which meant turning to the left at the main
corridor. Would her eyes adjust by the time she reached
that corridor? Getting as close to the wall as she could,
she felt her way along.

As she reached the blank space she believed to be
the intersecting corridor, she was about to turn when
she was attracted to a tiny horizontal sliver of light in
the distance further down the hallway. Slowly she went
toward that crack of light, trying to remember where
she was precisely and what was in that part of the
house. Stairs leading to the basement were closed off by
a door to keep the cool dampness from rising into the
rest of the house. When she reached the light, she sur-
mised that it was coming from beneath the door to the
basement.

What perverseness of her nature made her compul-
sively want to yank the door open and investigate? Her
curiosity had gotten her into trouble many times before.
Still if she thought something were amiss and did not
look into it, it would haunt her until she knew what was
behind it. Were she to go to her room, she would most

likely sit and worry about that light through the night.

Open, the door revealed a flight of stairs, lit by a single small torch in the basement hallway. Not great light, but enough to expel darkness. The wooden steps made slight squeaking noises beneath her feet, causing her to move with extreme caution.

At the foot of the stairs, she tried to remove the torch from place, but it would not move. Peering down the corridor, she could see distant blackness in each direction. Quietly, gathering her breath along with her wits, she stood, back against the wall, and listened for the tiniest sound. Nothing coming from above. Why had she not gone to Mrs. Sharlock's room and had a look in on her? At least then she would know if the old house had been abandoned or not. And what if Mrs. Sharlock were not in her room? She had to stop thinking such things.

A faint sound as of faraway laughter. It was difficult to tell from which direction it came. When it came again, there was also a mumbling of words. She determined to go toward where she thought the sound to be.

Before long she walked out of light, gradually penetrating darkness again. The basement was cold and damp, creating a clammy atmosphere. Fear. Pounding pulse beats so loud that they echoed in her ears. Surrounded by darkness, she had almost resolved to turn back, give up the quest and race to her room as quickly as she could, when she perceived a tiny glow of light coming from a distance ahead of her. She had never investigated the basement area, not having had a reason to do so; hence, the region was unknown to her. She had not even given thought to the fact that there was a mysterious nether locale at Merrihew Manor.

Forward. The sound of mutterings filtered to her and

she could distinguish that the voices she heard were those of men. Men? What men?

The glow disappeared as if a door had been closed to shut it from spilling into the hallway. The voices became indistinct.

As Joanne moved further into the corridor, she kept her eyes down in hopes of spotting light seeping under a door. Nothing.

The hallway seemed interminable as she inched over it. Certain she would reach an end or a turn before long, she continued. Although her eyes had become used to the darkness, she saw nothing. Time to go back. Perhaps it was only her imagination that had made her think she heard laughter or saw escaping light. Perhaps—

Suddenly a door was jerked open about twenty-five feet behind her. Voices of men and that of a woman. The soprano squealed and, rushing madly, plunged into the hallway. From where Joanne stood, the silhouette was that of a young woman and she appeared to be completely naked. She screamed again and ran into the darkness. Ribald laughter came from within the room and the door was pulled almost shut, leaving only a crack of light stabbing into the hallway. Seconds later Joanne collided with the young woman, who had run headlong into her. Joanne was knocked aside. The lass, whom Joanne determined was indeed in a state of undress, was so startled that she let out a bloodcurdling scream and ran beyond Joanne farther into the darkened area.

As Janne fell against the opposite wall, she touched against several kegs, barrels and boxes. Calculating, she constructed a barrier of the aforementioned containers with a narrow path on either side.

Once the barricade was constructed, Joanne squeezed around it and went to the door. The muffled sounds had continued through the construction period, now they had tapered off. Perhaps one of the speakers had gone elsewhere.

At the door, she pushed it enough that she could see in. The room was poorly furnished, mostly odds and ends of discarded furniture. An old table and several mended chairs, a candle on the table. A man was slumped in a large chair to the side. She could only see the back of his head. He appeared to be passed out. No doubt the reason the conversation had ceased.

Soon the approaching sound of footsteps. Again she pushed the door to widen the scope of vision. Startled, she beheld a man clad only in a translucent pair of briefs and the headdress she had seen the principal man wear at the magic ritual. No doubt in her mind that the headpiece was shaped to represent the head of a goat. Then it was not wrong that the word *warlock* had come to her. On the man's feet were a pair of hairy boots, fashioned in the design of a goat's cloven hoof. He carried a large jug, which he sat on the table.

Seeing that the other was barely conscious, he strode toward him in an attitude of accentuated masculinity. "Wake up!" he commanded in a hard voice, which, although it had a vaguely familiar timbre, Joanne could not recognize as one she had heard. "You owe me money, you drunken animal, and I intend to be paid for services rendered." He jerked the man to his feet. "Do you hear?"

After shaking the drunken man several times, his tormentor flung him back into the chair and proceeded to fill a large cup with wine. The liquid, which must have been cold, revived the other with startling effect.

"Oh, I say, what the devil's going on!" the man shrieked as he attempted to push to his feet.

"You're not going to pass out on me," the satanic creature said, "until you pay me that which you promised." He jerked the man to his feet again and turned him about.

Joanne could see, despite the wine streaming down over his face, that the man was Lord Henry Weston. As the man in the goat's head and boots maneuvered around, preparing to toss another cup of wine in Lord Henry's face, she could see that he was thickly muscled with an imposing physique. He appeared tall. She speculated that he was constructed similarly to Jim Cornhill; although, since she had not had intimate experiences with men, that same build could be properly obscured by fancy clothing, the likes of which Matthew Bienville wore. Still the voice did not go with either man; but it could have been disguised too for the sake of Lord Henry Weston.

"I don't have the money with me," Lord Henry groaned.

"Why not?"

"I carelessly forgot it."

"But it was all arranged, you fool!"

"I had difficulty getting away from the Constable," Lord Henry mumbled drunkenly. "Besides, I don't have to pay for the kind of girl you brought here."

"You weren't paying for her," the man in the mask stated. "That was only a little added amusement for your pleasure."

"Where has she gone?"

"Never mind that. You were to have brought me five hundred pounds."

"I don't have that kind of money available," Lord Henry insisted.

"Then you will see that it becomes available, unless you wish to be exposed as the murderer of Sara Cornhill and the Ornby girl."

"I didn't kill them."

"You don't *remember* killing them, Lord Henry. I saw you and there were others."

"I can get you three hundred pounds."

"As a starter," the other said. "But my fee doesn't end with a mere five hundred, Lord Henry. I should say it will soar into the thousands, unless—"

"Unless?"

A maniacal laugh. "Ah, that. Well, we'll see about that anyway, won't we, Lord Henry?"

"See about what?"

"Finding a way to prove that I am a Merrihew and entitled to the Merrihew estate. I have papers, signed documents. I can prove who I am."

"Who are you, sir?" Lord Henry asked, weaving as he attempted to focus on the person before him. Joanne could see that he was wearing what appeared to be a long nightshirt.

"You will know in time when the arrangements for my inheritance are made."

"If you are a legitimate heir to Merrihew, why the devil do we have to go about this silly game? Can't you just openly prove yourself?"

"That is a matter we're going to work out together, Lord Henry, long after this murder business is over."

"I didn't kill anyone," Lord Henry persisted, then suddenly stuck his head forward. "Did you?"

"Did I?" A diabolical laugh. "Since it's between you and me, Lord Henry, yes, I did kill the girls. I admit this now, only to let you know that I am ruthless enough to do the same to you if you don't do as I tell you."

"But if you killed the bloody girls, why must I pay you to keep quiet about the fact that I killed them."

"You don't know whether you killed them or not. You were drunk both times. I'm not working alone in this matter, you know. I have able assistance."

"By Jove, I can't for the devil figure where you think you have a case against me."

"Shall I start giving evidence to the Constable?"

"You have evidence?"

"Yes. Sufficient."

"Damn me! Pull that blasted contraption from your face and let me see who you are!" Lord Henry shouted.

Lord Henry was pitched back into the chair where he had recently been. "You may never see my face, Lord Henry, unless I have you in such a circumstance that my identity to you would not make any difference."

"What the devil are you up to, then?"

"Money, Lord Henry, and the Merrihew property, which is rightfully mine."

Lord Henry's assailant pulled his arm back, fist doubled in preparation of dealing the poor man a powerful blow in the face.

Joanne could stand it no longer. She screamed. "Don't! I heard you say you are the killer!" Quickly she squeezed beyond the barricade and ran as fast as she dared into the darkness.

"Her!" the man in the mask exclaimed. He did not bother to punch Lord Henry, instead he flew as rapidly as he could toward the door. In the hallway, he called, "Where are you?"

Joanne's running footsteps gave her away.

Moments later a loud clatter of barrels, kegs and

boxes. The man screamed several curses. Knocked off balance, he fell and the kegs rolled atop him.

Joanne ran wildly forward, uncertain of what lay ahead, but positive that she was running for her life. She only hoped she had screamed in time to keep Lord Henry Weston from any more of the man's abuse.

The corridor vee'd and she ran into the point between the two. Dazed and only softly hurt, she pushed herself back and went to her right, staying close to the wall and feeling her way. Behind her there were scuffling sounds —maybe the man fighting off the barrels. She did not wait to investigate, but hastened head-on into the unknown.

CHAPTER TWENTY-THREE

Completely turned about and confused, Joanne leaned against a cold wall to catch her breath. The frantic running had exhausted her, and the accompanying fear had propelled her into a degree of confusion that made reality seem an impossibility. Red terror flashed in her mind and every tiny nerve reacted in a chain response until she was overcome with a terrible prickly sensation of apprehension. Breath hot in her throat, uncontrolled trembling, a sinking dread in the pit of her stomach made her feel queasy. Why had she not gone directly to her room and bolted the door?

Inching her way toward what seemed to be oblivion, using the wall as a guide, she passed several doors in that endless tunnel. Trying the knobs, she found them stoutly locked. Her hands were perspiring; no matter how many times she wiped them on her skirt, that irritating feeling would not leave.

Finally a doorknob turned, the door pushed open with her weight. Intense darkness. Her eyes now accustomed to abject darkness saw nothing in that cavern of blackness. Dared she enter? Moist chills scampered along her spine. Against her better reason, she penetrated the room despite the sensation of imminent danger that might be awaiting her.

Almost upon entering, she tripped over a large object, then a second, losing her balance and falling in a sprawled posture. She pushed herself to her knees and crawled back to the objects that had tripped her to discover a pair of large, mud-encrusted boots. On an impulse she put them along side her own foot. She had seen boots of that size only on one person: Jim Cornhill. There was no mistaking the scent about them, they had surely plodded through many pastures.

She put her own foot inside one of the boots while still wearing her shoe. The shoed foot wobbled around in that enormous object.

Crawling about until she could find something to use to help herself up, she touched a chair. Feeling that it was not layered with dust, she assumed that it had been sat upon in the not too distant past. Pulling herself up, she sat. A rush of ease came over her with the alleviation of physical strain. She realized how very tired she had become.

After several seconds of just relaxing, if such were actually possible in that place, she began reaching her hands out, searching for any object that might be close by. A table. Round. Fairly sturdy. A candle upon it, alongside which were matches. The flicker of light bothered her eyes. The candle lit, the tiny glow covered the top of the table, nothing more. Taking the candle, she rose, and, holding the light high, attempted to survey the room. She would have to move around with the candle to actually see what lay beyond the perimeter of the glow. On impulse, she went back to close the door before she began her investigation.

The room was principally used for storage as many of the other rooms of the house were. Joanne wondered why her Uncle Alexander allowed so much useless junk to remain, when it should have been discarded years ago. Perhaps he never bothered to inquire into these basement rooms. Or maybe it did not disturb him since it was out of sight. She really did not know her uncle well.

Her uncle? Why a sudden curious thought? What about her uncle? He was in Europe somewhere with Susannah—probably in Paris. Wasn't he? She found a suit of gentleman's clothing, typical of the style Alexander Phenwick wore. She was of the impression it had recently been about a person. Why did she have that perception? Even the shoes were there.

Alexander Phenwick was her father's brother, older by slightly more than a year. Peter was the gregarious son, the instigator, not unlike her own brother Joshua; while Alexander was the solemn one, serious, studious, like her brother Prentise. She had observed many characteristics about her uncle as being similar to those of Prentise. He was not garrulous, although he was pleasant and made minor contributions to most conversations. Lex had studied Law at Harvard and graduated in the middle of his class with no particular acclaim. Edward Phenwick, Lex's uncle, had originally planned that the boy should take his place in his Boston law firm. Lex did so, but soon discovered his interest in law was not that intense. He acquiesced to his cousin, Andrew Ornby, married

Susannah Phenwick and took off for England to handle
the family's interests in Medallion Enterprizes there.

Other clothing. Some old and dusty. Worn uniforms
once used by the domestics. Four sturdy black dresses
of the same size, no doubt once occupied by Mrs. Sharlock.

The candlelight beamed into a horrifying face. She
squealed and nearly dropped the light. A grotesque mask
with glistening eyes appeared to be almost lifelike. The
head was in the shape of an animal with horns. The
mask, or one similar, she had seen first at the magic
ritual, then in that very basement, worn by the person
tormenting Lord Henry Weston.

A dreadful thought. She hurried back to where the
suit of gentleman's clothing was waiting. Putting the
candle on a box, she examined the clothing carefully. In
one of the pockets she found a small silver box with
the name "Alexander" etched on it. The box contained
tobacco dust particles. A card was in the vest pocket,
inscribed "A. Phenwick." She put the clothes back as
they were as best she could. Her heart was pounding
loudly, pulse erratically thudding in her ears.

The candle flickered out. She dashed quickly to the
table for the matches. Lit again, she carried the few
matches with her. What further was she seeking? She
examined the large boots that had tripped her. No mistaking those, she had seen Jim Cornhill wearing a similar
pair.

A closet. She pulled the door open. Ragged articles
of clothing were hanging there. Evidence of rats, perhaps other vermin. Old shoes on a shelf, partly gnawed
away. She had to think, to arrange facts in her mind and
reason out the situation.

As she was about to return to the first chair in which

sho sat, she heard a thud against the door. Dashing for the closet, she extinguished the candle just as the doorknob began to turn. Seconds later the door shot into the room. The figure in the goat's head mask lunged in. He went directly to the table. Hands groped about the top. He did not find the candle nor the matches he had left. Going to the side of the room, he found one match. Before he lit it, he inhaled deeply and perceived the aroma of burnt candle wax. Someone had recently been in that room. He struck the match. From her hiding place, she could see the unmistakable physique of the man she had seen twice earlier.

The man began to remove the mask, but it was so large and encompassing that the operation required two hands. He took the moments of matchlight to glance about in the corners of the room. Starting for the clothing in which Joanne had found Alexander's engraved snuff box, he got halfway before he hesitated. Again he examined the table for matches. The light was gone.

"Someone's been here," he muttered in a thick whisper. "Taken my candle." Heavy grunting as he removed the hoof-shaped boots. "Can't run in these damn things."

Joanne heard the skidding of chairs over the floor, hurried movement, the closing of the door. Then silence. Instantly she was ready to spring forward, before she realized he might have set a trap to catch her. She waited, her hearing set to the tiniest sound. Terrible apprehension filled her that the man was still in the room, by now his mask removed, sitting in wait for her to show himself. The anxiety became unbearable as she remained motionless in place, forcing herself to breathe slowly, noiselessly.

Again she thought of her Uncle Alexander and finding his clothing in that basement room. Was it possible

that he had left Susannah in Paris after her first concert,
perhaps on the pretense of having urgent business matters in London? He could stay at his apartment in the
city, coming at night, if need be, to Merrihew Manor
where he could prowl about at whatever he had to do.
Suppose he had killed Sara Cornhill. If she was the type
of girl even her brother acknowledged her to be, she
could entice a man such as Lex into a romantic situation; later perhaps attempted an extortion plot. After
all, he was known to be a wealthy man. Sara could have
threatened exposure to her brother. Or perhaps Lex had
become bored in all the long hours he had to sit about
waiting while Susannah practiced the piano. Out of boredom he may have investigated the local customs and,
having the intelligence and know-how, quickly set himself up as head warlock for a coven of faithful followers.
She thought that would be a relatively easy accomplishment with money behind him.

What could be a better way to turn suspicion from
himself than to kill one of his relatives and place her
in an identical position as Sara's body when it was
found? He had a perfect excuse: being in Paris at the
time, which would also take earlier suspicion from him.
Lex had mentioned interest in theatrical performances,
perhaps in companies and actors. A simple job to disguise himself with makeup: a false beard and moustache, heavy eyebrows, unusually shaped eyeglasses, a
different style of clothing. The pieces fit together too
nicely.

Five minutes had past. No sound, not even the scurrying of little creatures. Mustering courage from she knew
not where, she stepped from the closet. Again she listened. Still nothing. She took a match and hesitated before she struck it. Holding it high, she could see nothing

unusual. She lit the candle and circled about the table
with it held high as she searched the room. At last she
breathed a sigh of relief.

Her attention was drawn to the discarded cloven-
hoofed boots, which were obviously especially made for
the warlock. The heel was raised over four inches, making the basic line of the boot appear like the foot of an
animal. Lifting one, she took it to the boot she identified
as belonging to Jim Cornhill. Effortlessly she was able to
insert the hoof-shaped boot into the other; the lift of
the heel made it possible.

Going again to the corner of the room, she examined
the clothing which she was certain to be the property
of her uncle. Nothing was missing. That would indicate
that the man—be it her uncle or someone else—was still
in an abbreviated state of dress. No doubt he would head
for the upstairs part of the house where he could find
other apparel and plan his escape from Merrihew Manor.
Still not fully convinced of her uncle's participation in
the mystery, and furthermore not wanting to, she found
it difficult to reach any other theory or conclusion.

What was she to do now? Wait longer? For what?
Yet, if she were to find her way back upstairs, might
she not encounter the man who was recently in that
room? Even more fear began plummeting through her.
If there were only some way she could get out of the
basement without having to go upstairs. She could make
her way to the stable and ride to Falcon Heath Castle,
or on to London for that matter. The feeling of being
trapped became oppressive and she knew she must
leave that tiny room before her imagination carried her
to extremes.

Outside the hallway was not quite as dark as she remembered it. Cautiously she moved along, touching the

wall as she went. She chose to continue in the direction
she had been going before entering the room. The candle was still with her, but she had snuffed it before
leaving. Did she dare to light it?

Ahead of her the darkness was pushed slightly back
with the soft glow of candlelight. Not moving, she
judged it was coming from a stationary place. Con-
ceivably it could be another torch in the wall. She went
toward it both with fear and anticipation.

CHAPTER TWENTY-FOUR

The light was not coming from a torch. As Joanne approached, she saw that a door was open and the glow was coming from within. A murmur of voices and movement. Obviously more than one person.

Suddenly the unmistakable face of Toby Albright, with the turned-up nose and other distinguishing characteristics. His eyes widened as he saw Joanne, not fully identifying her. He ducked back into the room and closed the door.

She had been seen. She was determined to get behind what was transpiring. Waiting at the door, poised to rap, the door was again pulled into the room, and she stared into the beefy face of R. Piedmont Stopp. He seemed as surprised to see her as she was to see him. Each stared incredulously.

"I can't say I was expecting you, Miss Phenwick,"

Stopp finally said, motioning for her to enter. "At least we were hoping for someone else. Come in. Come in."

"Inspector Stopp! What are you doing down here?"

A single lantern was burning on the table. Other lanterns were about the room. Faces were staring curiously at her.

"Inspector Stopp is here with the rest of us, Miss Phenwick," Constable Jones interjected. He was seated on a barrel, a pewter cup of wine in his hand.

Alister Tweedly was standing near Constable Sedley Jones. As usual his blouse was open and his clothing seemed remarkably tight. His smile was awkward, like a small boy caught at something he should not be doing.

"You weren't at the stable when I returned from my ride," Joanne stated, directing her remark to the groom. "I left Jack tied outside. I'm surprised that you left your post."

"He did so at my bidding," came a voice from behind the door. "Alister, you had better continue the watch in the corridor."

Joanne recognized the familiar voice and spoke before she turned. "Matthew? Matthew Bienville? It *is* you."

"Good evening, my dear," Matthew returned. Was his voice cold because the other men were present, or had there been a change in his attitude?

She wanted to run to Matthew, to touch him. She needed close physical contact with someone she had deep feeling for. Yet he remained reserved and his attitude held her back.

"What is happening here?" she questioned, now looking back to Stopp.

The large inspector smiled. "We hope we have baited a bit of a trap here."

She turned to Matthew. "And you, Matthew, are you part of the bait?"

Now he smiled that lovely smile she dreamed about. "My dear, I think there is something you must know. I have deceived you in a sense."

"Deceived me?"

"Only in a sense," Matthew corrected. "I am everything that I have claimed to be—that is, professionally speaking—yet I am something more."

"Something more?" Joanne cocked her head. "I don't understand."

"Among other of my accomplishments," he related, "I am also a private investigator—very private, very exclusive and very expensive. I was privately hired to investigate the murder of Sara Cornhill by a man whose identity must remain anonymous for the moment. Only today did I present my credentials and make myself known to Inspector Stopp and Constable Jones."

"And it came as a bit of a shock to us," Jones commented. "After all, Bienville was our prime suspect, especially in the case of your cousin's death. And we were working on establishing a motive for killing Sara Cornhill."

"I might still be the guilty party, Constable," Matthew said in jest. "You have only my word and credentials that I am who I say I am." He turned to Joanne. "There is still some question in their minds because I refuse to divulge who has hired me. I have taken a solemn oath in that matter, and must not reveal his identity until he is completely cleared in the case."

"Why have you all assembled down in this specific room?" questioned Joanne.

"It's a trap," Jones reiterated.

"My assistant, man and trusted friend, Joply, is out

flushing the culprit down into these parts," Matthew explained. "We believe the murderer is involved with a group of persons who practice a weird sort of ritual similar to witchcraft. Individually I have interviewed many of the participants, who freely speak of such activities. Up until about a year and a half ago, these peasants had a relatively harmless form of recreation —disregarding moral standards, of course. Then a rather persuasive individual appeared, claiming he was a full-fledged warlock and intended to take over the group as their leader. This new leader arrived in disguise and always presented himself in such a way. Intimidating the people, they feared they would be burned at the stake for practicing witchcraft if they refused to participate in the rites he brought them.

"Sara Cornhill, a girl lacking in even a semblance of intellect, was a communicant in the strange ritual. Somehow she discovered the identity of the practicing warlock. Perhaps she tried extortion. That we may never know. Something like that must have been the motive for destroying the girl."

"Even if that person, the—what did you call him—the warlock were her own brother?" Joanne inquired, applying a little bait of her own.

The men rustled uneasily. That was not the theory they had earlier been asked to accept.

"That is quite possible," Matthew replied, seizing the opportunity to present another theory that had occurred to him.

"It is?" questioned Jones.

"How do you figure that?" Stopp asked, smoothing his moustaches with his index finger.

"Suppose Cornhill discovered his sister in the coven?" Matthew speculated. "After all, he was hiding behind a mask. Then Sara found out it was him. A threat. She was killed to quiet her. But Jim had a murder on his hands. So he killed a Phenwick girl for the sole purpose of making it appear as if another murderer were loose. Then he came to Merrihew and became acquainted with Joanne, convincing her along with the rest of you in the village that it was all a plot to make it appear that he had killed his sister and Miss Ornby."

Joanne stood defiantly staring into Matthew's handsome face. "Suppose I wasn't convinced. I don't believe Jim Cornhill is the murderer."

"Who else could it possibly be?" questioned Stopp.

There was accusation in the look she gave Matthew. She turned to make her statement to Constable Sedley Jones. "My uncle, Alexander Phenwick."

Everyone spoke at once.

Joanne then explained the hypothesis she had considered before, embellishing it slightly, presenting a fairly convincing argument.

"She makes sense, Bienville," Stopp exclaimed after hearing Joanne out. "Still I should think you would attempt to protect your relative. Isn't his life more important to you than the likes of Jim Cornhill?"

"Is it?" Joanne asked. "I am quite fond of my uncle. He is my father's brother and they are alike in many ways. Still if he killed Adriane and Sara Cornhill, what sympathy can I have for him?"

"Lord Henry Weston was earlier entertaining our man," Matthew informed, "playing his part after arranging with him to procure a local girl for him this evening—a girl from the coven. That same lass is in the next room fully clothed now. So far all is going as arranged."

"Lord Weston is playing a part?" questioned Joanne.

"Yes, that of the lecherous old man that he is," Matthew explained.

Joanne related the conversation she had recently overheard between Lord Henry Weston and the mysterious man in the goat's head mask.

"Extortion?" Piedmont commented. "Then this person must have had reason to believe that Lord Henry might have killed the lasses himself."

"That was planted information," Matthew explained, "that was gotten to this warlock person through devious means of my own to force him to show his hand. Lord Henry has long been a trusted friend of mine. He was the first I let in on what I was doing to discover a solution to this crime. That was before Adriane Ornby's death." He turned to Joanne, stepping to her. "As to your uncle being—"

The door swung open and Toby Albright came leaping in. "Someone's cumin'. I could hear his footsteps."

Matthew stepped to Joanne. "Will you help us, Joanne?" His hands touched her shoulders and the familiar excitement went through her.

The lamps were turned down, leaving only the one on the table with a faint glow.

"I want you to believe that I am very fond of you, Joanne," Matthew continued, "and that I do not think you will be in great jeopardy assisting."

"What do you want me to do, Matthew?"

"Stand here behind the table with the lantern glow in your face," Matthew instructed, guiding her into position. His touch alone was compelling. "The light is low, you may not even be recognized, but you will attract his attention. Once he's in the room, get into the corner. We'll close the door behind him, holding pistols on him."

"I understand," she said softly.

Silently they waited. Seconds passed, then minutes.

"Are you certain you heard footsteps, Toby?"

"Positive."

After a still longer period of waiting, Stopp stepped to the hallway, his ear cocked for sound. A short while later he scurried back into the room, whispering that now he heard footsteps. They each took their places, the door partly closed.

The footsteps got closer.

Joanne was filled with excitement, not completely free from fear. She trembled a bit and had to lock her jaws together to keep her teeth from chattering.

In a moment a large shadow lurched to the doorway. The man was blouseless, bare to the waist. Candlelight reflected off his perspiring hairy skin. A large hand thrust forward at the door and the man strode into the light. It was Jim Cornhill.

"Ay, lass, what do ye be doin' here?" he asked, gasping as if he were short of breath. He appeared rumpled and unsteady as one does when emerging from a fight. His look was that of an animal who has conquered another animal and come to take the feminine prize. Opening his arms he went toward her. "Ay, lass, 'tis me."

"No, Jim! Go back. It's a trap!" Joanne screamed.

The door slammed closed. The big man looked confused as he glanced about at the men coming toward him.

"All right, Cornhill," Matthew said as Jim continued to move toward Joanne until his arms were about her, "unhand the lass. We all have pistols."

Slowly Jim disengaged himself. He pivoted about, taking in all the faces. The large hand swiped across his face. He leaned on the table as Constable Jones poked his pistol barrel.

"Ay, 'tis like th' lot o' ye, ain't it?" Jim broke into uproarious but somewhat mocking laughter.

Joanne lifted the lantern from the table and held it to examine Jim's feet. "No! You have the wrong man. I was with Jim earlier this evening. He was wearing these boots then. The man I saw with Lord Henry Weston wore other things upon his feet."

"I ain't got but th' one pair since someone stole me others," Jim confessed.

"How long ago were they stolen?" Stopp questioned.

"Nigh two weeks ago," Jim replied.

"Where's your blouse, man?" questioned Matthew, annoyed at the announcement that Jim had been with Joanne earlier that evening.

"I got it tore off me durin' a fight just now," Jim informed. "I were fightin' with a man who had a goat's head mask over his head. A bloody rough opponent, he was, too."

"Where is he now?" Jones asked.

A thick hand rubbed over Jim's brow as he gasped again for breath. "Down th' hallway, he is. There's a room what he went in to put on some clothes."

"Who is he, could you tell?"

"Nay, lad. I weren't that curious, since I knew ye all was down here somewheres. Ay, I know about th' back entrance into this basement. That's how I finally found me way in."

Stopp was the first to the door. "Come along, men, and we'll have a look."

"You couldn't tell who it was?" Joanne whispered to Jim.

"I got me suspicions."

"Come along," Matthew ordered, "we will *all* go."

"Whatever ye say, mate," Jim returned, pushing Joanne ahead of him.

The man was in the same room where Joanne had remained in hiding. She recognized the boots, the clothing belonging to her Uncle Alexander. Stopp, the first to arrive, had prudently covered the lower part of the unconscious man's body. Toby had been sent to fetch wine.

. Stopp, with the assistance of Matthew, removed the large, grotesque mask from the man's face. Alister brought the lantern close. A gasp of recognition sounded at once as if on cue.

"There's your culprit," Stopp announced. "One, Cyrus Quigg."

"Quigg!"

"Quigg?" Joanne asked. "I can't believe—"

Toby arrived and was ordered to throw the wine into Quigg's face.

Quigg tugged at his tied hands, tried to kick his bound ankles. "Why are you all looking at me like that? I have just as much right as anyone to be here. I'm a Merrihew!"

"You?" questioned Joanne.

"I'm a Merrihew!" Quigg screamed. "I'm a Merrihew! I'm a Merrihew!"

More wine was thrown in the man's face and he coughed in reaction.

CHAPTER TWENTY-FIVE

Cyrus Quigg did indeed have documents proving that he was a distant member of the Merrihew family. What he had failed to realize was that Augusta Phenwick, the only direct Merrihew heiress, had made arrangements for full title of the property after the deaths of her parents. By paying specified monies to the government, she redeemed the improverished estate for her own, thus disengaging any ties that previous members of the Merrihew family might have.

The constable, with the aid of Joply, took Quigg into custody, with plans to transfer him the next day to London.

Lord Henry Weston, it was revealed, had a reputation for being a notorious womanizer, with special fancies for young girls in their teens. He had a rendezvous with Sara Cornhill, and paid her well for the encounter the very day of her death.

Since no money was found upon the unfortunate lass, a possible motive of robbery was suggested by Lord Weston to Inspector Stopp. When Stopp learned that Quigg had been in the local tavern that same evening, spending freely, he became suspicious. The second point that aimed Stopp in Quigg's direction was the way the butler walked with seemingly little pain after complaining of severely bruising his toes the night before. He well might walk properly while in the presence of others, but when clear of their sight, would surely resort to a limp—if indeed he had hurt his foot.

Joanne confirmed that she had heard Quigg's confession made to Lord Henry, when the latter claimed to have been acting as if he were in a drunken state.

"Yes, I admit it was all a trap to get Quigg," Stopp assured his listeners, who included Matthew, Lord Henry and Joanne. "I'd checked with Ira Cornhill, don't you know, and he had admitted to making several pairs of boots for Quigg. He stated, too, that Quigg had been on his premises prior to the murder of Sara, and shortly after that time, Jim's spare pair of boots were missing. I thought it a curious set of circumstances."

"I must admit I didn't suspect Quigg in this crime," Lord Henry commented, "but I knew the man was up to something when I discovered he spent a great deal of time with my wife when I was away. And since I'm notorious as a philanderer, that gave the old boy quite a bit of time with Lady Genevieve. There's no accounting for some people's tastes—and I'm referring to Quigg's."

"Had you any inkling then," questioned Stopp, "that Lady Genevieve was the one encouraging Quigg to establish himself as a Merrihew heir?"

"No. Can't say that I did."

Mrs. Sharlock brought a fresh pot of tea. Joanne served.

"Now, Matthew," she said, handing him a refilled cup, "can you disclose who employed you in this matter?"

Matthew smiled broadly. She had never seen him look so handsome. "It was your Uncle Alexander."

"Uncle Alexander?"

"He would not abandon Susannah on her tour," Matthew related, "but he knew that his innocence had to be proved. One of the first things I discovered upon arriving here after their departure, to hold suspicion to a minimum, was that Lex's clothing was being disturbed in his absence. That led me to believe that one of the household staff was involved."

"You suspected Quigg, too?"

"Yes, but the scene had to be played out," Matthew said, "to let the man ultimately show his hand. Last night, after I left you at the Prince Edward, Joply and I drove back here and managed an extensive amount of investigation. Quigg felt free to act with everyone away."

"How did you know Quigg would come to the basement?" asked Joanne, fascinated by the process of deduction.

"Because he indirectly arranged to have Lord Henry meet him there. The time he scheduled proved to be after the hour we knew the magic ritual to be over. Since he was out of the house, he did not realize that you were away, or if he did, he probably assumed you were gone for the evening as you had been the night before. He got a bit reckless on that point, since he apparently thought you no threat."

"Then how did Jim Cornhill happen to be in the basement?"

"His explanation," Piedmont replied, "and we might as well accept it, was that he had come looking for his boyhood friend, Alister Tweedly, with whom he often visited at the inn. Finding him and Toby Albright away, and your horse tied outside the stable, he became suspicious and went to investigate. Alister had told him about the back entrance to the basement and, when he found muddy tracks leading in that direction, he followed his instincts. I believe Jim Cornhill was also suspicious of Quigg and had been looking for that one bit of evidence to prove him right."

"How innocently I sat in this house," Joanne stated. "I could have been killed, too."

"We felt you were perfectly safe," Stopp said, "because of your natural intelligence. Apparently Quigg had appealed to Miss Ornby's sensual nature to lure her from the room the night of her disappearance. A plain girl with no apparent admirers is vulnerable to such an approach, more so than a pretty lass. Basically I feel Quigg had too much respect for you."

"Uncle Alexander hired both of you men, Mr. Stopp, Matthew," Joanne mulled, "and did not tell me about it?"

"A man as wealthy as your uncle hires many men in secret," Lord Henry informed. "That is one of the ways he remains wealthy."

Lord Henry Weston left with Inspector Stopp. They would go to Falcon Heath Castle, where the inspector would probably spend the night, to return to London early the next morning.

"Do you want me to leave tonight, now that you know the truth of my reason for being here?" questioned Matthew as he stood by the fire warming himself, studying the blaze.

Joanne crossed to where he was standing. "Was it necessary to play on my emotions to accomplish what you were after?"

He turned to her. "I confess, at first that was my intention, Joanna. But after knowing you only a short while, I found I was reacting with my heart. I don't have to do this private investigating work, you know. I have other income—a considerable amount and potential for more. But I wanted to impress your uncle. I was serious when I said I wanted to get in with Medallion Enterprizes. I exaggerated when I said I needed you as an entrée to your uncle. That was just part of the play in which I was acting."

"The play? Acting?" Joanne gazed into his handsome face. The smile was intriguing. Something magnetic shot from him, drawing her to him. "Matthew, teach me to become an actress. You're most accomplished, I can tell."

"I apprenticed once with Colton-Smith," Matthew confessed, "but quickly discovered it was not a lucrative profession. I still find it fascinating as a spectator."

She threw her arms around him. Tiptoes. Kissing with impact and promise, she nearly knocked him off his feet. "We're going to London first thing in the morning and I'm taking a suite of rooms at the Prince Edward. I'll not wait until Uncle Alexander and Cousin Susannah return before I learn to become an actress."

Matthew looked at her a moment at arm's length. "Do you love me, Joanna?"

"I don't really know what love is, so I can't say. Do you love me?"

"I'm very near to it, Joanna, very near. I've never come so close before in my entire life."

"Don't rush falling in love, Matthew," she said with a determined grin. "I want us to become good friends first, to know each other, to share important things. Then we can talk about love."

"And marriage?"

"I could not marry unless I was absolutely certain I was deeply in love."

"But you and I in London—"

"Oh, I didn't mean we would live together—just nearby."

She kissed him again. There was hope and promise and the beginning of love . . . but only the beginning.

Joanne was up early the next morning. The day was bright with a gray overcast. The haze would burn off by noon with the promise of a lovely afternoon. From her window as she gave Mrs. Sharlock instructions what to pack and how she wanted her things arranged, she saw the familiar figure of Jim Cornhill lumbering over the lane leading to the stable. Oddly, he was not on a horse. Periodically he would glance up at the mansion with a pensive expression, stop, stare, then move forward.

Explaining she would return shortly, Joanne left the room and flew down the stairs, ultimately to bound out the side carriage entrance. Her skirts rustled with the accelerated movement.

Jim stood watching as she ran toward him. "Oh, Jim, I'm glad you came. I wanted a word with you before I left."

"Do ye be leavin' Merrihew Manor then?" he asked, husky-voiced.

"I'm going to London," she informed. "The country is nice, lovely, but can't you feel the chill in the air. Winter is coming and I would be stranded out here in this big, drafty mansion all alone. I need to be where people are and excitement is."

"Ye're very pretty, lass, ha' I ever told ye that?" he said simply.

"I think I got the impression you thought that."

"Well, I do. I think about ye quite a bit, I do. An' it keeps me from thinkin' 'bout other things," he explained. A playful boyish expression twinkled his eyes and his big hands reached to clasp her shoulders. "I'm right smitten with ye, lass. I can tell because ye are always on me mind."

She hugged him, placing her head on his massive chest. "Oh, Jim! Jim, we're just friends, you and me. Good friends. I'm not a country girl. I was born in the city, practically raised in the heart of Boston. I become restless and bored away from people."

"But if'n ye were to marry an' have babies," he suggested, "then ye'd have plenty to keep ye occupied."

"That's just it, Jim, I'm not ready to either marry or have children. I have too many goals I wish to accomplish before I get myself into a fix like that."

"Ha' ye so little respect for marriage?"

"I respect marriage for others, not for myself at the present time," she returned. "Please try to understand."

Jim gazed at his feet in the narrow space between the two of them. "When is it ye're a-goin' into London?"

"Within the hour."

"Am I nay to see ye again?"

"I'll be back from time to time to visit my uncle and cousin," she said. "And if you're ever in London, I hope you'll look me up. I'll be staying in the same hotel, the Prince Edward."

"Ay, but in London ye will be occupied with others."

"I'll always find time for you, Jim." She kissed him full on the mouth and he reacted with the strength of his body. When the kiss ended, a strange reaction came over Joanne. She swallowed hard. "You really meant that, didn't you?"

"Ay, lass, that I did."

Again she put her head to his chest. She was trembling. Physically she respnded to the man; she had fr the time they first met. Within her a voice said that s could love him, be fulfilled by him in many ways—bu not in the way she wanted most. Tears. Biting of lips t gain control. Slowly she pushed herself from him.

"I must go now, Jim. I've packing to finish and there are arrangements to be made," she chattered, searching for words, thoughts, anything that would get her mind from the emotions of the moment.

"Ay, 'tis best, lass, 'tis best. I was a bit o' a dreamer, that is all. 'Twill pass, like one season passes from another. Ay, 'twill be no time at all before I be about me regular activities."

One final kiss, catching him off guard and planted on his cheek. "You will come and see me in London, won't you?"

"Ay, lass, o' that ye can be certain."

She stared emotionally into his coarsely handsome face. Determinedly she turned and ran back to the mansion. Jim stood watching until his eyes became so clouded with moisture he had to look away. As he turned to stroll back up the lane, over the hill and through the forest to home, Alister Tweedly and Joply brought out the carriage and horses.

Traces of vapor like threads of steam hovered about Merrihew Manor as the carriage pulled away. The top was laden with luggage. Mrs. Sharlock stood at the door, modestly waving, which was a lavish display for her.

Jaspar and Alonzo ran barking after the carriage, attracting the attention of other dogs who came to join in the farewell song. Soon the geese, too, were hissing, wings up, necks stretched forward.

Joanne glanced back from the window of the vehicle. Mrs. Sharlock was already out of view as were Alister ___dly and Toby Albright at the stable. The mon- ___ mansion, as gray and foreboding as ever, was ___ ___ading into a memory.

___urned back to Matthew seated close beside her. ___niled reassuringly as she placed her hand on his ___squeezed.

London!" he shouted, and bent to kiss her on the ___eek.

"The theatre!" she returned, and squeezed his hand significantly again.

THE END